THE SECRET OF THE SILVER LOCKET

Orphan Grace Walker will come of age in 1925, having spent years as companion to the daughter of an aristocratic family. Grace believes her origins are humble, but as her birthday approaches, an encounter with young American professor Harry Gresham offers the chance of love and a new life. What could possibly prevent her from seizing happiness? A silver locket holds a vital clue, and a letter left by Grace's late mother reveals shocking news. Only Harry can piece the puzzle together . . .

JILL BARRY

THE SECRET OF THE SILVER LOCKET

Complete and Unabridged

LINFORD
Leicester

First published in Great Britain in 2014

First Linford Edition
published 2015

A catalogue record for this book is available
from the British Library.

ISBN 978–1–4448–2440–7

1

The sound of raised voices drifted downwards as Grace climbed the staircase leading from Seymour House's spacious entrance hall. She knew this latest quarrel between Lady Carmichael and her daughter Rowena was entirely predictable.

'This one will be no better than the rest,' Rowena snapped from inside her bedroom. 'I wish you'd realise I'm not ready to become someone's meek little wife. Never, ever, Mama!'

Pausing outside the door, Grace couldn't resist smiling. Meek was the last word to describe the Honourable Rowena. Taking advantage of the sudden silence, she knocked, calling, 'May I come in?'

'Yes, of course.'

She found mother and daughter standing on opposite sides of the yellow-and-white bedroom. Despite the sunshine streaming in, each wore a stormy expression.

'Good morning, your ladyship.'

'Grace, thank goodness! Can you try and talk sense into my daughter? She's obviously lost what little she already had.' Lady Cressida Carmichael sailed majestically towards the door, grasped the handle and turned to deliver one parting shot.

'I shan't insist on your joining me at luncheon with my friends, Rowena. But I shall expect you to be ready, suitably attired, downstairs, at precisely six-thirty.' She glanced at Grace. 'I hope that won't spoil any plans you might have for your night off, my dear.'

'Not at all. I'll make sure whatever Rowena plans to wear is ready well in time, your ladyship.'

'I'm pleased someone understands this evening's importance. I'd like to see my daughter in the pale blue silk but I suppose that's too much to hope.' Lady Carmichael left, her heady perfume still lingering.

Rowena glared at Grace. 'Simpering blue silk, more like! Think yourself lucky no one expects you to make a good marriage.'

Grace didn't answer but pushed a loose tendril of dark hair behind her left ear.

'Oh, I'm sorry,' wailed Rowena. She hurried across the floor and flung her arms around her companion. 'That was a stupid, thoughtless thing to say. You know I think of you as my friend, not a servant.'

'Not everyone in this house sees me as that, Ro.'

Rowena stepped back. 'Is someone making life difficult for you? They'd better not be!'

She looked so fierce, eyes glittering and fists balled at her sides, that Grace laughed out loud. 'I'm very lucky with my life, considering what might've happened to me after my mother died. No, I only meant I'm dithering as to whether going out with Matthew is sensible or not.'

Rowena sank on to the bed, patting the space beside her upon the white satin counterpane. 'You know I'm madly

jealous? Not one of those chinless won-
ders Ma throws at me looks anywhere
near as delectable as Matthew.'

'It's a pity he has a chip on his
shoulder about his status. Looks aren't
everything, are they?'

'But he has cheekbones to die for!
Surely you agree it helps if a prospective
husband doesn't too closely resemble a
goldfish?'

Grace sat down. 'Put like that, how
can I possibly argue? Matt's asked me
several times to go out with him and
now I've agreed, I wonder whether he
thinks I've been — well . . . '

'Ooh . . . playing hard to get?'

Grace felt heat flood her cheeks. 'It's
not an expression your mother would
approve of but that's precisely what I
meant. What if he asks me to walk out
with him?'

'You should say yes, of course. Have
some fun! You've far more chance of
having fun with Matt than I have,
dining with some namby-pamby son of
an earl.'

'You might be pleasantly surprised. Anyway, sometimes we all have to do things we wish we didn't have to do.' Grace smoothed creases from the bedspread. 'Would it be so very difficult to surprise your mother and make an effort to be charming to your escort tonight?'

She watched Rowena's eyes narrow. Had she pushed the boundaries of friendship too far? As Rowena's official companion, Grace also undertook many lady's maid duties. It might be 1925, with the world fast changing, but Seymour House still gave the impression of a well-oiled steam engine serenely towing a string of gleaming carriages. Unless you counted the occasions when the vivacious daughter of the house ignored the signals and went rattling off along the wrong track.

'I suppose you're right. You usually are. But how I wish I could change places with you this evening.'

'You know that can't happen,' said Grace gently. 'Instead, we need to talk

5

about which of your dresses you plan to wear. If you don't fancy the pale blue, shall I change the trimming on your emerald green? Maybe it needs to be a more dramatic contrast than the cream?'

Rowena's eyes sparkled. 'That would be wonderful, if you're sure you don't mind going out to buy ribbon. I'd come with you but I doubt there's time before Ma's hairdresser gets around to me.'

'Don't worry. I'll wash your hair then go straight to Selfridges.'

'Ma always says blue and green are seldom seen. But d'you remember the colour of the ocean that time we were in France, watching those adorable little yachts bobbing in the harbour?'

'I do. The right shade will remind you of the Mediterranean and I'll buy enough ribbon to allow for threading some through your curls.'

Grace prepared to wash Rowena's golden hair ready for Lady Carmichael's stylist to create the waves and ringlets appropriate for a demure debutante. She was hardly likely to forget the holiday to which Rowena referred. Lady Carmichael had taken both girls to visit some major European cities. While staying in a popular French spa resort, Rowena had fallen in love with a dark-eyed waiter working in their hotel. Grace had needed all her skills of tact and diplomacy in juggling her overprotective, anxious employer with the high-spirited, often rebellious Rowena.

Fortunately this short-lived crush fizzled and flared unnoticed by her ladyship, who, while walking along the promenade, had encountered a former acquaintance from her own debutante days and become ecstatic at the prospect of gossipy catch-up sessions. When her ladyship and the girls progressed to the next stop in their tour, Rowena had mooned about for a while, something her mother put down to an indisposition caused by foreign food, and certainly nothing a brisk walk couldn't remedy.

Grace left Rowena with her hair swathed in a towel and carried the green gown off to the workroom where she and housekeeper Emma sewed and ironed the vast variety of garments required to maintain the elegant appearances of the lady of the house and her daughter. Soon she was flying down the back stairs and through the tradesmen's entrance into Berkeley Mews, towards the hustle and bustle of Oxford Street.

Grace enjoyed the feel of the sun on her face as she continued on her way, passing the local butcher's shop and giving the proprietor a wave as he glanced from beneath the brim of his beribboned boater. He called a cheerful greeting but Grace wasn't buying succulent lamb chops or a juicy gammon joint today. She was bound for the big department store so favoured by her ladyship and her cronies. At least Rowena was taking an interest in what she'd wear for her dinner engagement, maybe even heeding Grace's words.

'Where are you off to this fine morning, then?'

Startled, Grace paused outside the fishmonger's to look up at Matthew, the household's under-chauffeur who also acted as valet or sometimes butler, depending on how Mr Alfred Hicks, his uncle, delegated duties. Matt wore a flat cap on his curly fair head and carried a bulky package tucked beneath his right arm.

'Selfridges,' she said. 'To purchase some ribbon, if you really must know.'

'Mrs Potter sent me to buy Dover Sole, thanks for asking.'

'You'd better get back while they're still fresh, then. Her ladyship's entertaining her best friends to lunch.'

'A witches' coven, is it? Woo woo . . . ' He gave a chilling impersonation of the Hound of the Baskervilles.

Grace did her best to keep a straight face, although she knew Rowena wouldn't have hesitated to laugh out loud. 'Don't be impertinent, Matt. It doesn't become you.'

He doffed his cap with his free hand, allowing the bulky package to shift slightly. Grace dived to rescue it and as she looked up at him, their gazes locked for moments before she stepped back.

'I must go. Try and get those Dover sole home before they turn into pumpkins!'

'Cheeky! We still on for the flicks tonight?'

'Yes, of course. I'm free as soon as Mr Hicks drives the family off to the Ritz.'

'I'd better wait outside the kitchen door for you. Uncle Alf'll skin me alive if he catches me hanging round the front entrance. We could see *The Thief of Baghdad* if you like. That Douglas Fairbanks bloke's in it.'

Grace glanced back at Matthew as she set off. 'It's fine by me. But please don't get any ideas about sitting in the back row.'

'No, your ladyship. Whatever you says, your ladyship.'

Grace hated it when Matthew teased her. She couldn't help the way she spoke, any more than he could disguise his East End roots. She'd been a young baby when her mother and father had taken up employment with the Carmichael family and she'd never known any world other than that of Seymour House. As a child she'd shared Rowena's tutors, though not required to attend dancing and piano lessons, much to Rowena's annoyance. Grace's way of speaking in no way matched her serviceable attire, though she knew her place — a place that frequently left her feeling as though she inhabited a no man's land between gentry and domestic staff.

She walked on, still agonising over the wisdom of accepting Matt's latest invitation. He was a nice boy and he'd asked her out several times before. She knew many people, including Rowena, would wonder what her problem was and why she didn't agree to walk out with him regularly. Grace knew that wouldn't be fair. Whatever lay ahead of her, she knew it didn't involve walking into the sunset with Matthew. His status didn't matter one bit to her, but her feelings for him were based on friendship and she must find a way to let him down as gently as possible.

In Oxford Street she stood outside the prestigious department store, admiring an eye-catching window display of mannequins wearing bejewelled and beaded cocktail dresses, before she headed for the haberdashery department. While she examined the spools and skeins of colourful ribbons, Grace pictured in her mind's eye the rich azure of the Mediterranean Sea sparkling in the sunshine. When a saleswoman hurried forward, a welcoming smile on her face, Grace felt comfortable, knowing the young assistant appreciated Lady Carmichael's custom and would treat a lesser member of the household with as much courtesy as she would Rowena or her ladyship herself.

'Good morning, Miss Walker. How are you today?'

'Very well, thanks, Miss Black.' Grace returned her gaze to the display, feasting her eyes upon the palette of colours. She saw every shade of pink, from fondant to magenta. Every colour green Mother Nature boasted, from palest almond to darkest moss.

'You have a marvellous selection and I'd like to see those two shades of blue on the right, please.'

Replacing the trimming slotted around the dropped waistline of Rowena's favourite gown wouldn't take Grace too long. Rowena was to accompany her parents to a dinner that evening, and on such an occasion Grace wouldn't expect to be included. Despite her qualms about Matthew's intentions, she looked forward to seeing the film, which she'd heard was highly entertaining. However, the thought of hurting and disappointing the young man was a different matter, especially as they so often came face to face in the course of their duties.

Retracing her steps, Grace arrived at Seymour House to find the Rolls Royce parked outside the front. Alfred Hicks, a man entrenched in the old-fashioned values and who retained enormous nostalgia for the horses and carriages of former times, stood polishing the already-pristine windscreen of the deluxe motorcar.

Tall, broad-shouldered and clean-shaven bar a neat moustache, he wore his chauffeur's cap and uniform with pride. Matthew must have inherited his golden hair from his Uncle Alf's side of the family.

'I can see myself in the paintwork, Mr Hicks!'

He looked up and smiled. 'It's a pleasure to keep a motorcar like this one looking good, Grace. I'm driving his lordship to his golf club this morning.'

Grace knew Lord Carmichael well enough to realise he'd doubtless awarded himself a few hours off from business affairs, to compensate for having to escort his wife and daughter to an evening function that couldn't possibly interest him. She also knew that if his lordship couldn't find a caddy, the resourceful Mr Hicks would oblige.

Head to one side, the chauffeur surveyed his handiwork. 'I don't suppose you know the cause of my nephew's sudden cheerfulness? Could it be you're the reason why I found him waltzing

Mrs Potter around the kitchen table just now? He's lucky she didn't set about him with her rolling pin.'

'Fancy,' said Grace, feeling even guiltier than ever. 'It's not for me to say, Mr Hicks. Now if you'll forgive me, I must find Miss Rowena before she sends out a search party.'

She disappeared around the side of the house, enjoying the thought of Mrs Potter, Kitchen Queen, responding to Matthew's dance invitation. The formidable cook unsuccessfully hid a soft spot for the young man and Grace could only hope Matt hadn't let slip his plans for the evening. There'd be enough teasing and grilling from Rowena without the domestic staff joining in.

As she closed the back door behind her, Grace heard the sound of Matthew's cheerful voice, followed by Mrs Potter's West Country burr, though she couldn't catch what they said. She also smelled the spicy whiff of freshly baked gingerbread but didn't dare linger, her mind

focused upon her sewing task. She tiptoed past the door to the stillroom, where
Matt was doubtless drinking a cup of
strong, sweet tea with the cook, and
rushed up the back stairs and along the
corridor to Rowena's room. She tapped
on the panelled door.

'Who is it?'

'It's me — Grace. May I come in?'

'No, no! Not just yet, Grace, please.
Did you buy the ribbon?'

'Of course. Do you want to see it? I
can pass it through if you open the door
a crack.'

'Is it the shade we talked about?'

'It is.'

'Then please go ahead with the work
and I'll see you at lunchtime. We'll have
ours in the little sitting room. In peace,'
Rowena added darkly. 'Emma said
she'd bring you some tea. Miss Phipps
and I have just had ours.'

'Thank you,' called Grace, setting off
again. Wasn't that just typical of Emma
— to think of her on such a busy
morning. Wondering what Rowena

could be up to behind her closed door, Grace arrived in the sewing room moments ahead of the woman who, as well as carrying out the duties of housekeeper and acting as maid to Lady Cressida Carmichael, provided a comforting and constant presence in Grace's life.

Plump, motherly and with the most amazing sunburst of curly red hair, Emma sailed into the sewing room bearing a tray upon which sat a chubby little china teapot complete with cup, saucer, spoon and slice of sticky gingerbread upon a tea plate.

'Emma, I'm utterly parched. I hope you realise you're truly an angel.'

'If I didn't know better, I'd think you kissed the Blarney Stone while you were out shopping!' Emma placed the tray upon the table next to the ironing board and picked up the pot ready to pour. 'Mind you, keep that dress at a safe distance. I brought the gingerbread because Miss Rowena thought you mightn't last until luncheon without something to sustain you.'

'She's being surprisingly co-operative today — except with her ladyship.'

'She's probably anxious for you to make a good job of her gown. Not that there's any doubt about that. Now, I'd better put your cup on the mantelpiece in case you knock it flying.'

Grace chuckled. 'If I do that, it'll be more than my life's worth.'

Emma eyed the package. 'Should I unwrap this and smooth out the ribbon while you eat the treat?'

'Please, Emma.'

'I've a damp flannel in my apron pocket. I'll not leave until I've seen you wipe your fingers clean.'

For once, Grace didn't mind Emma talking to her as if she were a five-year-old. The family cook's baking skills were such that she could take basic ingredients, throw them up in the air and mix them into a symphony. Mrs Potter had cooked for far grander families than the Carmichaels and still found time to bake a big enough batch of gingerbread for the staff to enjoy a taste too.

'What's all this secrecy over Miss Rowena's hair? I wasn't allowed to step inside her room.' Emma began unfolding the ribbon. 'That Miss Phipps came and whisked away the tray.'

'I've no idea.' Grace sipped her tea. 'There's sufficient ribbon there if Rowena wants some woven through her ringlets.'

'I'm surprised the hairdresser didn't ask you to take a length to her. Are you getting a trim today?'

'Only if Miss Phipps has time for me.'

'Your hair suits you, scooped up like that, but if you miss the boat and need me to wield the scissors, you've only to ask.'

'Thank you.' Grace swallowed the last luscious crumbs and took the damp flannel Emma held out.

The older woman regarded her affectionately. She'd taken over as substitute mother after Grace's mother died of the Spanish Flu, leaving the thirteen-year-old alone in the world, Grace's father having perished in the trenches towards the end of the Great War. The couple had arrived in London from Scotland when Grace was a babe wrapped in a shawl, and they obtained positions with Lord and Lady Carmichael on the strength of glowing references provided by their former employers in Edinburgh.

Emma had been much relieved when Lady Carmichael called the serious young girl to her and explained Grace would never lack a home and that Emma would tutor her in the duties necessary to her position. Emma, much more than a mentor, had also provided laughter and cuddles and helped Grace learn to live with the loss of her darling mother. Fortunately Rowena loved Grace like a sister — in some ways better than a sister — and the two girls joined Rowena's parents at table for family meals and accompanied them on outings, except the more formal ones.

'I meant to tell you, I've finally agreed to go out with Matthew,' said Grace as the housekeeper turned to leave.

The woman who knew her so well gazed at her without comment.

Grace hesitated, seeing something in Emma's eyes she didn't quite comprehend. 'You don't think it's a good idea, do you?'

Emma smoothed her hands down her apron front. 'I'm wondering what changed your mind. You're not the type of girl to encourage a young man's attentions unless you feel it's the right thing to do.'

Grace bit her lip. 'I'm afraid that if I don't go out with him, he'll only keep on asking. And now I've agreed, maybe that'll be the end of it. He probably only wants to boast to his friends, if I know Matthew.'

Emma stared at her. 'That young man worships you, Grace. You'd do well to bear that in mind before trampling all over his feelings.'

Grace sat down and began to unthread the old ribbon. 'I wish you'd told me that before I agreed to go out with him. I'm not so insensitive that I haven't been worrying about the possibility of hurting him.'

'Surely you knew how he felt? Can you not see the way he looks at you and has done for a long time?'

'He teases me a lot, that's for sure. I don't know about special ways of looking.'

'No,' said Emma. 'You obviously don't.' She shook her head. 'Oh, how I wish your mother was still alive!'

'And you think I don't wish that too?' Grace's eyes were bright with unshed tears. 'But we can't bring her back. The past is in the past.'

'Except when it comes back to haunt you.' Emma rushed from the room.

Grace, puzzled by the anguish she'd seen on the older woman's face, stared after her, knowing better than to follow.

* * *

Matthew pushed his back against the sturdy wooden chair, tipping it so it balanced on its two hind legs.

'I'll thank you to sit like a gentleman at my table, young Matt!' Mrs Potter glowered at him, one hand poised to cut a slice of gingerbread.

'I beg your pardon, I'm sure.' Hastily he adjusted his position. 'I wouldn't want to risk your displeasure, Mrs Potter.'

'Cupboard love,' she said. 'I wasn't born yesterday.'

A slow grin spread across Matt's face as he watched the cook's lips twitch.

'Soon as we've had our elevenses, I'd like you to check the dining room.'

'Again? Do you think someone's broken in and messed things up since Uncle Alf gave it the once-over?' At once he knew he'd spoken out of turn and held his breath, awaiting the reprimand.

But Mrs Potter seemingly hadn't noticed. Instead, she passed him his plate. 'Even the best of us can forget something when there's other things on our mind.' She sat down opposite Matthew and spooned sugar into her tea.

'What sort of things?' He took a mouthful of gingerbread and closed his eyes while he munched. He was counting the hours until he and Grace walked out together for the first time. With his dream about to come true, his attention wasn't exactly focused on whatever his uncle may or may not be contemplating.

'I'm sure it's not for me to say.'

Matthew opened his eyes again. 'Do you think my Uncle Alf's worried about something? If so, he hasn't said a word to me.'

'Nor has he to me.' She didn't need to say the word 'unfortunately'. Matthew was well aware of the family cook's avid interest in everybody else's business and also knew her bark was worse than her bite.

'So what's the problem?'

'Did I say anything about a problem?' She leaned across the table. 'Truth is, I caught him reading a paper yesterday.'

'Well, there's a rum thing. I hope he wasn't checking the racing results when he should've been on duty.' Matthew ducked. Just in case.

But Mrs Potter still looked thoughtful. 'Mr Hicks was taking a tea break, if you must know. I came up behind him and couldn't help noticing he was looking at a photograph of a property.'

'What kind of property?' Matt was intrigued. Uncle Alf must have a long stocking by now, but he still wasn't anywhere near approaching the seaside bungalow stage.

'A lodging house or small hotel, by the looks. I couldn't see whereabouts because he closed up the paper in a flash and started talking about some play or other.'

Matt frowned. 'He might be thinking about his holiday. He usually has some time off before the season's parties and dinners get going.'

'Of course. It's just . . . I don't know. Something in my water tells me there's change afoot.'

Matt burst out laughing. 'Oh, I'm sorry, Mrs Potter. You know I don't mean to be rude but I can't imagine Uncle Alf changing his ways, I really can't.'

'You mark my words, Matthew my lad. Without mentioning no other names, I think Mr Hicks has plans and he's keeping his cards close to his chest.' She rose and placed both hands on the tabletop as she looked him in the eye. 'Don't you go saying anything, mind. Not to Grace, nor anyone else. I wouldn't want Mr Hicks to think I was a gossip.'

'Heaven forfend such a thing,' said Matt gravely. Plans? Surely not. He thought the chances of Alfred Hicks escaping his ordered routine within the London household were very slim indeed.

2

Upstairs, Grace's nimble fingers flew as she tried to make sense of Emma's strange remark. Had she meant her own past coming back to haunt her? Or was it Grace's she'd hinted at? Not that Grace could think of a thing that might have caused Emma's sudden consternation. Either way, there was nothing either of them could do to alter things. She knew Emma had been Grace's late mother's best friend. Could it be she felt in some way to blame for the tragic ending to Amy Walker's life? Surely not, given that the particularly vicious influenza epidemic had continued until it succeeded in wiping out a huge section of the population.

She reminded herself each one of Rowena's exquisite garments cost far more than she could even dream of affording, should she be forced to fend for herself. She happily accepted hand-me-downs to wear when accompanying Rowena on excursions, and her ladyship ensured Grace always possessed two good-quality, demure charcoal-grey or navy-blue dresses for everyday wear.

Grace had almost finished weaving the azure ribbon through the openings in the luxurious green fabric when the workroom door burst open. Deliberately, she kept her attention focused upon the painstaking stitches necessary to hold the final section of ribbon in place.

'Well, what do you think?'

'I think you've come for the blue ribbon so Miss Phipps can complete her work of art.'

'Wrong,' said Rowena, sounding gleeful.

Grace snapped off the end of thread and glanced up. 'Oh, my goodness, Ro — what have you done?'

Twirling around, Rowena began singing a few bars of the Charleston song that was currently all the rage, before bending and placing each of her hands upon each dimpled knee and crossing them back and forth. Her gleaming blonde hair, newly shaped in a flapper-style bob, swung either side of her lovely, oval face.

Grace rose, carefully placed the green gown upon a hanger and hung it on the rail. Rowena straightened up, grabbed her friend's hands and whirled her around what space remained available as a dance floor. Her enthusiasm was so infectious, Grace could do nothing else but join in.

'So, do you approve?' Rowena released her breathless partner at last.

'It suits you, no doubt about that.' Grace walked around her, admiring the sleek coiffure. 'Miss Phipps has excelled herself, but what on earth will her ladyship say?'

'She'll either have to put up with my new look or leave me at home and tell everyone I'm indisposed. Either way, I couldn't care less. Don't you think, at 20 years of age, I should be able to choose my own hairstyle?'

Grace selected her words carefully. 'Well, yes, but wouldn't it have been better to mention it first?'

'Definitely not. Ma would've ordered the hairdresser to stick to the old, boring style. Now listen. Miss Phipps is waiting in my bedroom. She says she'll bob your hair too. But you have to get a move on because she's due round the corner at a house in Manchester Square at two o'clock.'

'Are you trying to get me dismissed, Ro?'

'Don't be silly. Ma would turn me out before she got rid of you!'

Grace couldn't disguise her delight. 'I must admit, it would be good not to have to put my hair up every morning.'

'If you change your mind later, you can always grow it back. Stick it in a snood or something until it's long enough to put up again.'

'All right. But how much will this cost? I don't like to think of her ladyship footing the bill.'

'Don't worry about that. Just come with me and be transformed. I bet Matt will adore your new look, especially if you wear that red-and-white two-piece costume.' She grabbed Grace's hand. 'While Miss Phipps works her magic, I'll go down the back stairs and wheedle a sandwich for her from Mrs Potter.'

'What if you bump into your mother?'

'That's hardly likely, is it? Not when she's probably, at this very minute, preparing to sip sherry with her terrifying trio of friends. Talk about a witches' coven!'

Recalling Matt's quip earlier, Grace threw her inhibitions to the wind and hurtled along the corridor with Rowena.

'That should settle into place nicely after your next shampoo,' said the hairdresser after she'd given Grace her new look. 'Why don't you take a peek at yourself in Miss Rowena's looking glass?'

Grace peeked and held her breath.

She couldn't remember when she'd last undergone such a change of style. Now her dark, glossy hair, swinging either side of her heart-shaped face, accentuated solemn, grey eyes beneath a feathery fringe. As Grace turned her head from side to side, Miss Phipps held up a silver-backed hand mirror.

'Now you can see what you look like from behind, Miss Walker.' She lowered her voice. 'In my humble opinion, you'd give any of those high-society flappers a run for their money.'

Grace chuckled. 'Goodness knows what her ladyship and Emma will say. But, thank you. I like my new hair. I like it very much indeed.'

* * *

After the girls ate together, Rowena went upstairs to read a novel she'd been given by a friend and which she'd told Grace must on no account be allowed to reach the hands of her ladyship. Grace collected the luncheon things and stacked them neatly, ready to carry the tray to the stillroom. She wondered, not without apprehension, what kind of mood Emma might be in, having rushed off earlier looking so strained.

She found Mrs Potter applying finishing touches to a luscious home-made trifle, adding crystallised violets and glacé cherries at the last minute so they didn't leach colour onto the whipped-cream topping. Emma was up to her elbows in soapsuds when Grace tiptoed past the busy cook and hovered in the stillroom doorway. The house-keeper turned to see who was bringing more dirty dishes.

'Grace! Is it really you?'

'It's definitely me. What do you think of Miss Phipps's handwork?'

'I'm not sure.' Emma didn't meet Grace's eyes. 'I . . . I'll need time to get used to it. I thought you only wanted a trim?'

'So did I, until Rowena persuaded me otherwise.' Grace found a space for her used crockery and shot Emma a worried glance. 'I'll give you a hand with these.'

'Thanks, my dear. I suppose this means Miss Rowena's sporting a similar hairstyle? Is her ladyship aware?'

'Not as far as I know. So it might be as well not to say anything when you next see her.'

'Matthew's clearing away the main course, as Mr Hicks is still swanning around the golf course with his lordship. So I probably shan't see her ladyship on her own until I help her dress for their night out.'

'I see. I'm sorry if you're missing Mr Hicks.'

'I'm sure I don't know what you mean by that!'

Puzzled by the instant rosy blush flooding Emma's cheeks, Grace hesitated. 'I only meant he's a safe pair of hands, and you must be wondering how well Matt's doing in the dining room without his uncle to keep an eye on him.'

'I wonder what Matthew will make of your new look,' said Emma, scrubbing at the prongs of an engraved silver fork as though her life depended upon it.

'That thought honestly hadn't occurred to me.'

'No? Well, we'll soon find out.' Emma straightened up, dried her hands and moved away so Grace could take her place. There had been a strange look in Emma's eyes — almost, Grace thought, as though the older woman had something important on her mind yet couldn't bring herself to speak it out loud.

'New kitchen maid, is it?' Matthew, his brown eyes sparkling with fun, deposited four empty wine glasses on the draining board beside her.

'Now Matthew, none of your cheek,' said Emma. She rolled her eyes, hearing the cook calling. 'I'm on my way, Mrs Potter. I expect you'd like me to take in the trifle next.'

Left alone with Matthew, Grace waited for another cheeky comment, but nothing was forthcoming.

'This is a surprise,' he murmured, coming so close that she detected the tangy scent of coal tar soap.

'I quite often help with the washing-up, as well you know,' she said, deliberately misunderstanding. 'It's all hands to the deck these days, Matt, in case you'd forgotten.'

'I hadn't forgotten, but I meant your hair,' he said. 'You look beautiful, Grace. Even more beautiful than you were before.'

'Get a move on, Matthew,' called Mrs Potter. 'Trifle's going through now. Mr Hicks saw to the glasses earlier and pudding wine's in there, in case you hadn't noticed. You pour while Emma serves dessert. Lord knows I try to keep up standards, though it's a hard job without enough staff to shake a stick at. 'twere a different matter in my last position.'

Matt winked at Grace. 'I'd better go before our dear cook has my guts for garters.'

Grace, still busy at the sink, couldn't believe Matt thought she looked beautiful. If Mrs Potter hadn't broken the mood, would he have tried to steal a kiss? Why hadn't she noticed the signals as Emma had? And what had made Emma lose her usual calm demeanour?

★ ★ ★

Grace clapped her hands together. 'You look like a movie star. Or I should say a fashion model?' She stood back to admire the full effect of Rowena in her finery.

The other girl turned slowly around, inspecting herself in the gilt-framed cheval mirror. 'My new hairstyle suits this dress, doesn't it?'

'Definitely,' said Grace. 'It's so fashionable you look as though you've stepped straight from the pages of *Vogue*. I can't believe your mother won't approve.'

'She's bound to find fault. She prefers much more formal wear for evenings, but I think I can get away with this outfit at the Ritz.'

'Who exactly is attending this dinner, Ro?'

'Several of Ma and Pa's cronies with assorted offspring. It's supposed to be an informal start to the formal start of the London season, if you see what I mean. I missed most of last year's functions, of course.'

Grace nodded. Rowena had fallen from a particularly frisky horse while a guest at a house party in the country and, much to Lady Carmichael's exasperation, had been laid up for many weeks and therefore slipped behind in the marriage stakes, as Rowena called them.

'So, are you to be partnered by anyone in particular? You said something about the son of an earl.'

'I'm told Lord Redvers Fountain, heir to the Carnforth Estate, is my beau for the evening. My mother has taken the trouble to find out his interests but goodness knows what we'll find to talk about. I despise country sports. I can't drive and I'm nowhere near as good as you are at hitting that silly white ball over the net. I doubt he cares about women's rights, and as for liking musical theatre productions . . . '

Grace giggled. 'You might be agreeably surprised.' She handed Rowena her stole.

'I'll let you know in the morning. Have a wonderful evening with the delicious Matthew.' Rowena looked at Grace, her head tilted to one side. 'You know, you look very pretty indeed. Even more so when you're blushing! If he kisses you, I demand to know all about it.'

'Rowena, you're incorrigible. Now you'd better go downstairs before her ladyship sends Emma to fetch you.'

'You might see me back in two minutes if Ma decides I'm not suitably attired.' She blew Grace a kiss and shimmied to the door.

Grace was ready for her outing but before using the back stairs to the kitchen quarters, she couldn't resist hovering on the landing, to be within earshot of Lady Carmichael's reaction to her daughter's new look.

Oddly, it was Rowena's father's deep, cultured voice she heard first. 'By George, my dear, you look very elegant. New dress, is it? Very nice indeed. Let me put that lacy thing round your shoulders for you. Doesn't our daughter look a picture, Cressida?'

Upstairs, Grace held her breath.

But instead of the tirade Rowena had anticipated, Lady Carmichael's opinion appeared to be as positive as her husband's.

'My goodness, Rowena, what a surprise! But I like the way your dress is trimmed. And how strange that you have had your hair bobbed. According to a friend of mine who knows the countess, her grace is wearing a new look too. Now let's not keep Hicks waiting any longer, shall we?'

Grace felt relieved that Lady Carmichael wasn't critical but it was ironic how Rowena had unwittingly jumped straight into her mother's good books. Whether she took Grace's advice and acted like a dutiful debutante should, would be a different matter.

It was a fine evening so Grace wore no coat over the smart costume Rowena had recently given her. She found Matthew in the courtyard wearing a dark jacket and trousers, his hair slicked down and, much to Grace's surprise, looking as nervous as she felt.

His face creased into a smile as he stopped lounging against the red brick wall of the recently constructed garage and hurried towards her. 'You look a treat and that's a fact,' he said. 'I'm sorry I'm only taking you to the Ritz picture house and not the Ritz Hotel.'

She laughed. 'I don't think I'd fit in there. The pictures will do fine, thank you.'

They fell into step, walking through the rear gateway.

'Funny to think my Uncle Alf's driving the family to the Ritz Hotel as we speak. You tell me you don't belong in high-falutin' places but just between you, me and the gatepost, don't you ever envy Miss Rowena her invitations to all them posh parties?'

'Not at all,' said Grace crisply. 'Often she has to sit through formal dinners with lots of courses, being bored by interminable tales of hunt balls and cocktail parties in the shires and what the French ambassador said to someone's Uncle Hubert last Tuesday night at the embassy.'

'Strike a light, if that don't prove you could be one of 'em!'

'One of whom?'

'There you go again. You talk like a toff, Grace. I only wish I could compete.'

Impulsively, she slipped her hand through the crook of his elbow.

Matt took a deep breath. 'Feeling sorry for us now 'cos I talk like an East End boy?'

'What's wrong with that? You speak very nicely and I don't hear Mr Hicks correcting you as he used to do when you first arrived. Are you trying to pick a fight before we've hardly got down the road?'

'If you really want to know, I'm

trying to make sense of your feelings for me, such as they might be.'

'That's very forward of you, Matthew Hicks.' Grace began to regret taking his arm but didn't wish to seem anything else but self-possessed.

'You may think it's forward but it's taken you more than a month of Sundays to agree to come out with me. To tell the truth, I've been thinking about you and me for the best part of two years.'

Her insides lurched alarmingly. This had all the makings of an embarrassing evening. She sensed Matt had been bottling up his feelings and decided to confess them sooner rather than later. How would she manage to sit next to him in the darkness of the cinema? Why was life suddenly becoming so complicated?

* * *

Beneath a ceiling garlanded with glittering chandeliers, Rowena glided demurely behind her parents towards the long table at the end of the dining room. Redvers was delayed and she'd declined to take her father's arm, rather enjoying the surprised stares of several dowagers seeing her walk confidently by minus an escort.

Suddenly there he was. She had company in the form of a tall young man with hair the colour of Mrs Potter's gingerbread and a Roman nose sprinkled with freckles across its bridge.

'My sincere apologies, Miss Carmichael,' said Lord Redvers Fountain. 'I've committed the cardinal sin of turning up late, thus causing you to walk unescorted towards the dining table. Can you ever forgive me?'

Rowena suppressed a chuckle and held out her hand for him to shake. He lifted it to his lips and kissed her fingers while keeping in step with her.

'You're forgiven, Lord Fountain but I wouldn't have blamed you, had you decided to cry off this evening.'

'Please call me Red. It's not my fault

my parents gave me a ridiculous name to match my hair.'

He offered her his arm. 'By your remark, Miss Carmichael, I gather you haven't been looking forward to this dinner either. I've only just returned from Paris, which is why I had to jump in a cab and follow on as soon as I'd made myself tidy. Did the old man explain?'

'The earl presented your apologies to my parents and me most charmingly.'

'The Honourable Miss Rowena Carmichael and escort,' Red told a hovering waiter.

A chair was pulled out for Rowena and once she sat down, her dinner companion remained standing until all the other ladies in the party were seated.

'That's a jolly pretty frock, Miss Carmichael,' he whispered to her. 'Most girls I'm partnered with look like parcels wrapped up with coloured strings.'

'You're allowed to call me Rowena,

but you might bear in mind that my own dress is trimmed with ribbon.'

'That's as maybe but it isn't that wiffly-waffly kind of stuff, all pale pinks and blues and twiddly bits.'

'Perish the thought, though my mother would have me in that kind of dress if I allowed her.' She glanced around the table. 'You're safe to sit down now, Red, if you can face having yet another beribboned skirt beside you.'

He chuckled and took his place. 'I can't believe we haven't met before.'

'I was presented to their majesties last season but very stupidly fell off a horse and injured myself.'

'You rode a horse into Buckingham Palace?'

Rowena giggled. 'Sadly, no. It happened down in Devon.'

He sighed. 'Our paths might have crossed before except I've been out of the country a lot.'

'Lucky you. I'd adore living in Paris.'

'Then let's run away together.'

'I doubt I could run far in these shoes.'

He made as if to peer beneath the table and she reached for his sleeve and tapped his arm with her shapely fingers.

Rowena gasped as he trapped those fingers with his right hand and squeezed them. 'People will wonder what on earth we're up to.'

'Let them.' He released her hand with reluctance. 'Tell me all about you. I want to know how many men I shall have to duel with before I fall swooning at your feet. I want to know why you'd like to go and live in Paris. Most of all, I want to know whether you'll accept my invitation to luncheon tomorrow.'

Rowena couldn't believe how excited she felt. Red was nothing like any of the young men she'd kept company with before. She felt he was more than a match for an impulsive, outspoken character like her. His unconventional good looks set her heart racing. Yet, how annoying to find herself following a path set out for her by her mother's and society's expectations.

'Come on,' urged Red. 'Live dangerously.'

The words were enough for Rowena to fall under his spell.

* * *

Grace sat beside Matthew in the stalls, totally engrossed from the moment the organ began playing a beguiling melody and the film's title flickered upon the screen. She knew they were about to watch an *Arabian Nights* fantasy but her eyes widened at sight of the ancient dream city of the East. A camel train wandered across the marketplace. Along came four turbaned flunkeys dressed in baggy pantaloons and braided waistcoats. They were carrying a canopied bed upon which reclined a bejewelled and veiled woman, fanning herself as though her life depended upon it.

Grace felt as though she was there in the marketplace, so lost in the story did she become. It wasn't until after the national anthem was played and they made their way to the foyer that Matthew took her hand.

'You enjoyed that, then?'

'Oh yes, thank you. I had a lovely time. Thank you so much for treating me.' She felt him squeeze her fingers and wondered what was coming next.

'When do you think her ladyship will want Admiral's Rest opened up?'

'I've no idea, Matt,' she said. 'Are you hoping you'll be working down there this year?'

'I'm due a turn but I don't fancy being separated from you if you're kept busy here.'

They walked on in silence, past the darkened bulk of the British Museum. Grace, secretly wishing Matthew would indeed be temporarily transferred to the family's holiday residence and solve her dilemma, strove to find the right words. 'Matt, I'm not sure this is a good idea.'

'What do you mean?'

'You and me. It . . . it's just that I don't think I'm the right girl for you.'

He let go of her hand as if her fingers had burst into flames. 'You think you deserve better than an under-chauffeur, don't you? Play your cards right and you might get yourself a teacher, even a doctor — is that what you're after?'

'I don't have anything in mind, Matt,' she said softly. 'Except I owe loyalty to the family for giving me a home all these years.'

'That doesn't mean they own you.' He stopped walking and grasped her elbows, turning her to face him. 'As soon as Miss Rowena's married off, you could go where you wished. Surely you don't want to spend the rest of your life running round after her ladyship? Because that's what'll happen, you mark my words. One of these days, Mrs Potter will hang up her apron for the last time and Emma will take over the job. You'll be housekeeper and lady's maid from then on.'

'How can you be so sure Miss Rowena will marry? She has a mind of her own and she despises every young man she's introduced to.' Grace almost let slip how interested Rowena was in the suffragette movement and how she attended the occasional meeting without her parents' knowledge, but decided against it.

'She'll bow to her parents' wishes all right. At age 20, they won't want her hanging around on the shelf much longer.'

'That's an awful thing to say.'

'The truth always hurts.' He released his hold.

They continued walking side by side although Grace realised more than ever how he and she were worlds apart.

'So what do you have in mind for my future? Should I be concerned nobody's trying to marry me off? Should I be afraid of having to live my life as an old maid?'

'It's none of my flippin' business,' muttered Matt.

★   ★   ★

51

Next morning dawned with all the promise of a sultry, sulky day to come. Matthew, instructed by his Uncle Alf to wash and wax both the Daimler and the Rolls Royce, stood shirtless in the courtyard, performing the mundane task, his mind anywhere but upon buckets of water and chamois leather cloths. If only he could erase Grace's image from his mind as effortlessly as he removed dust from the vehicle's bodywork and squashed insects from the radiator grille. Last night he'd hoped would prove to be the first of many outings with the young woman he so admired, but she obviously didn't feel the same. Now he felt cross with her for going out with him in the first place and with himself for having crowed like a cockerel to his mates, so delighted was he at the prospect of escorting her to the pictures.

As for the questions she'd asked, he hadn't wanted to anger her by giving his honest opinion. He was biased, of course, but he was too proud to plead with her to give him a chance. Getting to know one another better, away from the curious gaze of family members, was what he'd enjoy. Who knew what might develop from a friendship? Determined not to show his disappointment and risk a scathing remark from his uncle, Matthew was carrying his buckets to the old water pump when he noticed a figure shifting from one foot to the other outside the gate, as if uncertain of her next move.

'Looking for someone, miss?' Matt called.

'Looking for a job, more like, mister.' The girl straightened her battered straw hat.

Recognising a Cockney sparrow, down on her luck yet still wearing a brave smile upon her face, he walked towards her. 'What kind of a job are you after? My name's Matthew Hicks and I work here.'

She held her hand out to him. 'I'm Polly Watts, and to tell the truth, I don't know what kind of a position I could fill until I tries it.'

Matthew wiped his right hand on his breeches and shook her hand as solemnly as he shook hands with his lordship when receiving his Christmas box each year. This girl had something about her, though he couldn't say for sure what it was.

She nodded towards the house. 'So is there any work going in this place?'

'What's this? Have you heard something I haven't?'

She shook her head. 'Course not! I'm trying all the big houses around the square. This one's my fifth but if there ain't nothing, I'll move on to the next.'

He watched the corners of her mouth droop and drew himself to his full height.

'I could ask if you like. Our cook — Mrs Potter she's called — often says she could do with another pair of hands around the place.'

Polly gasped. 'Oh, but I couldn't cook proper. Not for posh people, I mean.'

'But you could peel spuds and gut

fish and wash up?'

She nodded. 'Do cleaning. Make beds. Hard work don't scare me.'

Matt unfastened the gate and beckoned her through. 'Best if I go inside first and put a word in for you. I can't promise anything but I'll do my best.'

He watched her eyes travel down his chest before she looked away in a hurry. Suddenly he remembered his manners. This kid probably hadn't ever seen a man's bare chest before. He stalked over to the wooden bench where he'd left his blue cotton shirt, grabbed the garment and shrugged his arms inside. 'Wait here,' he called to Polly before disappearing through the door leading to the domestic quarters.

Matthew found Mrs Potter sitting at the kitchen table, consulting her ancient cookbook.

'It's not time for your tea break yet, your lordship,' she said. 'Not that I'm not looking forward to hearing about your night on the town.'

He ignored the remark, accustomed

to her teasing. 'There's a person outside asking about work. What d'you reckon?'

The cook's brow furrowed. 'What kind of a person? There's rumblings about taking on someone to help out here and down at the coast but it'd have to be a lass.'

'Well this person's called Polly Watts and I reckon she's barely done with school.'

Mrs Potter groaned. 'And where will I find time to train a youngster from scratch, pray tell?'

'She don't expect to do nothing fancy. She could be kitchen maid or housemaid, or both if that's what's needed. Strikes me she's desperate to find something.'

He watched the cook considering. At last she nodded. 'I'd suppose you'd better bring this Polly inside then. I'll have a chat with her before I call Emma. What are you waiting for?'

Matt stared at her. Should he mention Polly's coffee-cream skin? But the girl had better manners than many of the other young servants around and about their neck of the woods. He'd let Mrs Potter make up her own mind. Suddenly he found himself hoping Polly joined the household. Despite her faded cotton dress the colour of weak tea, and the little straw hat with a floppy brim, he thought she'd fit in well. Also, he'd no longer be the most junior member of staff if this girl were to be taken on.

3

Upstairs in Rowena's room Grace pulled open the curtains and turned to face the bed. Its occupier opened one eye and closed it again.

Rowena groaned. Loudly. 'Ooh, my poor head.'

'Drink your tea while I run you a warm bath,' said Grace. 'How much champagne did you guzzle last night?'

'Only a teeny amount.' Rowena dragged herself into a sitting position. 'But oh my word, Grace, we had such fun! A little gang of us went on to a club Red knows. We danced and drank cocktails and I didn't get home 'til two. Poor Hicks had to wait up for me.'

'Goodness. Well, he's very loyal and I didn't hear you come in so I imagine you're safe. And there was you, dreading the evening.' Grace noticed the pretty green dress abandoned on the back of an armchair and picked it up to drape over a hanger.

'I didn't imagine I'd get on so well with my escort.' Rowena sipped her tea.

'Ah.'

'Oh, Grace, Lord Redvers — or Red as his friends call him — is utterly divine! I'm torn between bliss at meeting such a delightful man and annoyance at how Ma's probably going to be thrilled when I tell her he's asked me out to lunch. He's only just returned from Paris after travelling around Europe so she'll be cock-a-whoop at the thought of stealing a march over the other scheming mothers. It's all too silly, of course. I've told her I have no intention of marrying anyone.'

Grace bent to pick up Rowena's jewelled satin party shoes, hiding a smile as she did so.

'Do you mean the invitation's for today? Is this a private luncheon he's planning? Surely he doesn't think your mother will allow you to spend time with him unchaperoned?'

'I've no idea. He won't tell me where he's taking me. Isn't it fun? He's so unlike any of those dreary oafs I've met so far. In fact, I think I might just have fallen in love!'

'I'd never have guessed.' Grace couldn't help smiling back at her. After all, she was Rowena's maid companion, not her mother. 'I'd better run your bath. I'll put in plenty of lavender salts and while you're in it you can decide what you want to wear for your rendezvous with Sir Redvers.'

'But how shall I do that when I have no idea where he's taking me?'

Grace stopped in her tracks. 'Would you like me to choose for you? It sounds as if you need to look casual but elegant for this young man. Nothing too frivolous, but pretty and practical enough to see you through a picnic if that's what he has in mind.'

'You're an angel. What on earth would I do without you?'

As she prepared the tub of scented

water, Grace mused over that last remark. There was no doubting Rowena's headstrong nature. Regardless of her opinions of marriage, if she decided to succumb to her new beau's advances, she wouldn't care two hoots for anything or anybody else. Matthew's words of warning echoed in Grace's head. The further Rowena progressed towards the goal of matrimony, which despite the young woman's protests, was inevitable, the closer Grace moved to a change in her own lifestyle. Would she gather the courage to move away from the security of Seymour House, wrapped in the knowledge that Emma had promised her late mother always to be there for her?

Maybe it had been wrong not to give her friendship with Matthew sufficient time for her to discover whether her feelings might possibly change towards him. Given her humble background, why should she feel this reluctance to settle for a young man whose vowels weren't as well rounded as hers? Had she turned into a snob? Considering herself to be neither fish nor fowl, Grace wondered whether she faced a life of loneliness, albeit her background equipped her perfectly for the role of travelling companion to some aristocratic lady.

When at last she went down to breakfast, she was horrified to find her employer already at the table and tucking into kedgeree.

'I'm sorry to be late, my lady.' Grace hovered, waiting to be invited to sit down. 'Rowena will be here soon.'

Lady Carmichael smiled. 'My daughter and other young things went off to a night club. I must congratulate you upon the clever way you trimmed that green gown, Grace. Your skills are so enviable, I shall have to take care one of my friends doesn't try to steal you away from us.'

Wondering whether she was receiving a veiled warning, Grace managed a wry smile and helped herself to cold ham and kedgeree. Breakfast was her favourite meal. The family served themselves and when, as today, his lordship was already at his office, conversation wasn't punctuated by snorts and grumbles over news items he so avidly absorbed from his daily pristine copy of *The Times*.

She was relieved when Emma entered the room.

'Your ladyship, I'm so sorry to interrupt your breakfast but I've been speaking to a young girl who's seeking employment.'

'Is this someone with whom you are already acquainted, Emma?'

Grace listened as her friend described how a girl called Polly had turned up out of the blue, asking for work.

Her ladyship buttered the remains of her bread roll. 'I haven't told any of you yet, but his lordship and I have decided it's high time Admiral's Rest is prepared for the summer.'

Emma nodded.

Grace knew the housekeeper would be expecting this announcement, even if it were imparted a tad earlier than previous years.

'You more than anyone else must know how short-staffed we are. If you approve of this young person, you have my permission to offer her employment, provided, of course, there is someone to provide a character reference. Presumably she could ask a school mistress or clergyman to vouch for her, even if she has no experience of a household such as this?'

'She's a churchgoer. I do know that.'

Lady Carmichael raised one elegant eyebrow. 'How refreshing. Well, there's the first hurdle dealt with. We should require her to live in, I think. Certainly for the first few weeks while she finds her feet.'

'Of course. She lives in Camden Town.'

'Really?'

Grace often needed to suppress the urge to laugh aloud when listening to her ladyship who on this occasion reacted as though Camden Town, a couple of miles down the road, was some far-flung outpost of the British Empire.

'I think she's a good girl,' said

Emma. 'It's a case of too many mouths to feed at home. Polly's clean and tidy, if a little shabby, and her manners are excellent. Oh, and she said her father is, um, African.'

'What about her mother?'

'Born in Hackney. Salt of the earth kind of folk, if I might say so, my lady.'

'Well, that's something.' Lady Carmichael dabbed her mouth with her linen napkin. 'The girl deserves a chance. She can learn the ropes with Cook for a few days while you and Grace are away at the coast.'

Grace exchanged glances with Emma. 'You want both of us to go, my lady?'

'Yes, indeed. It's not ideal, I agree, but we need Admiral's Rest ready as soon as possible and if I send you two with Mr Hicks, I know you'll carry out the preparations to my liking. Mrs Potter's more than capable of instructing this new girl in basic duties. Ask Cook if she'd be kind enough to sleep here for two or three nights. Rowena's bound to complain, of course.' Her ladyship inclined her head in Grace's direction.

'What am I bound to complain about, Mama dear?' Rowena appeared in the doorway.

'I'm afraid you'll have to lose Grace for a few days, darling. It's time to open up our summer residence and I need her to help Emma and Mr Hicks.'

But as Rowena approached the breakfast table, Grace noticed a telltale gleam in her eye. Whatever the daughter of the house's plan might be, Grace wouldn't be around to watch her carry it out.

'When would you like us to set off, your ladyship?'

'As soon as possible, Emma. Some time this afternoon would be good. I imagine you'll need two or three full days down there before returning.'

* * *

'Is that the lot now?' Alfred Hicks took Grace's black valise from her and wedged it inside the boot of the Rolls Royce.

'I believe so.' Grace looked at Emma. 'I shall sit in the rear seat and keep an eye on our packed lunch.'

'Oh but you should sit beside Mr Hicks,' protested Emma.

Alfred cleared his throat. 'May I suggest you two ladies change places when we stop for refreshments?' He ushered his passengers into the vehicle, stepped onto the running board and settled behind the wheel.

Grace sneaked a swift glance through the rear window as they moved towards the gateway. Matthew stood, face impassive, watching their departure. She raised her hand to wave but lowered it again, seeing him turn quickly away. If he chose to sulk, that was his lookout, but she couldn't help wishing he'd find someone else to be the object of his attentions.

Mr Hicks wasn't attired in chauffeur's uniform, as no family member was making the trip. He wore a flat tweed cap on his fair hair and a sober suit and white shirt with a dark grey tie. His hands, in tan leather driving gloves, rested lightly on the steering wheel as he manoeuvred the big car through the morning traffic, deftly avoiding darting pedestrians, wobbling cyclists and a variety of motor vehicles progressing along Oxford Street.

'There's one of the new two-man taxis,' said Alfred as they crawled past the John Lewis department store.

'That doesn't seem very polite, not allowing ladies to travel in them,' said Emma.

Grace giggled as Emma turned to wink at her. She leaned forward. 'It's a good job Miss Rowena's not with us. She'd have something to say about that.'

'Do they really think having smaller vehicles will help solve the traffic problems?' Emma turned her head to gaze at Alfred's profile.

Grace noticed the older woman seemed in no hurry to look away again.

'I suppose they'll try various measures. People complain about the motorcar taking over but we all have to move with the times. I took my turn working with horses but, in my humble opinion, driving motorcars is far better than putting up with the mess all those animals made of the streets.'

Grace knew the chauffeur-cum-butler had taken some convincing when his lordship decided to purchase a car. She wondered what age Mr Hicks might be. He had to be well over 40, probably nearer 45. She knew he'd worked for the family for ages. He couldn't be that much older than Emma. His and her generation had endured far more hardship than even an orphan like Grace could imagine, though she knew from personal experience how it felt to lose a loved one who'd been sent overseas to fight.

She turned her thoughts to more cheerful matters, leaning forward as Mr Hicks steered them towards the suburbs and the roads became less congested.

'It's good news about the new girl, isn't it?'

'I should say.' Emma glanced across at Mr Hicks. 'Did you meet her?'

The chauffeur slowed down to allow a chimney sweep to cross the road. The sweep touched his cap to them, teeth gleaming in his soot-streaked face.

'Maybe he'll bring us all good luck,' said Alfred. He turned right at the next junction before answering Emma's question. 'I didn't make her acquaintance but Matthew swears she'll be all right. For the life of me I don't know why he considers himself such a judge of character.'

'If Polly survives a few days under Mrs Potter's supervision, she'll be more than all right, I reckon,' said Emma.

Alfred cleared his throat. 'It's to be hoped everything goes smoothly while we're away. Being short-staffed is something we're used to but with the three of us down at the coast, it's not going to be easy for the rest of them.'

'You've trained Matthew very well

indeed,' said Emma. 'Don't you think so, Grace?'

'Of course. He seems very competent.'

'Well, I shouldn't say this, as he's my own kin, but I'm pleased with the way he conducts himself,' said Alfred. 'His lordship has no complaints and that's the main thing. Between the three of us and the gatepost, I just hope Matt won't get itchy feet and look to better himself now he's got a few years of experience under his belt.'

They drove on in silence. Grace, who had no desire to answer questions about Matthew's character and possible prospects, tried to think of another subject to raise. But there seemed no end to Mr Hicks's pronouncements. Watching his expression reflected in the driving mirror, Grace found herself lip-reading as she heard him mutter, 'I hope to goodness he's not making a fool of himself.'

'I beg your pardon, Mr Hicks. I couldn't hear what you were saying.'

Alfred coughed. 'Thinking out loud, Emma. Nothing for you to concern yourself with.'

To Grace's relief, Emma took the situation in hand. 'I'm hoping these next days won't be too arduous for us all. Of course I know it wasn't possible, but we could've done with Matt's assistance.'

'I'm sure we'll manage,' said Grace quickly. 'Mr Hicks, if necessary, you can ask the farmer for his son's help with moving furniture we need to clean behind.'

'If it'll speed us up it'll be worth a few bob. Her ladyship's given me a list of items she's decided ought to be shifted to different places.'

Grace hid a smile. That, she could well imagine. She knew the three of them would have their work cut out. But as their journey continued and they began to see fields rather than row after row of terraced houses with sooty brick-work, she decided to put questions about Rowena's latest romantic entanglement, not to mention her own awkward situation over Matthew, out of her mind. She loved the seaside and had many happy memories of beach games and swimming with Rowena. They'd liked to collect different varieties of shells and take them home to play with. Life had become a little more complicated since those carefree days.

When Emma turned around, her eyes asking a question, Grace realised what she had in mind. Fortunately there were fields either side of the road.

'I expect you could do with a break, Mr Hicks,' she said. 'Could you stop when it's convenient, please? I have a flask of tea with sandwiches and cake when you're ready.'

'No sooner heard than accomplished.'

Alfred drove on until he found a suitable place to park. He wound down his window, letting in the sweet sound of birdsong.

'I think I'd like some refreshment before I take a little walk,' said Emma.

'That sounds a very good idea.' Grace untied the package provided by Cook and offered the pile of sandwiches to the two in front.

They munched in silence, enjoying the fresh air. Grace got out of the back and placed the flask of tea and three cups on the grass verge so she could pour without danger of spilling anything on the upholstery.

When Emma clambered over the stile in search of privacy, Mr Hicks disappeared discreetly in the opposite direction. Grace tidied away the remains of the impromptu picnic and climbed up to perch upon the top of the gate.

Mr Hicks returned before Emma made an appearance. 'Grace, I know this is none of my business but both you and Matthew are important in my life. I don't like to see either of you unhappy.'

She stared at her shoes.

'I take it the boy's hopes have been dashed?'

'Your concern is appreciated, Mr Hicks, but I don't think I should discuss Matthew's feelings, even with his uncle.'

He took a step back. 'I understand. I'm sorry for speaking out of turn.'

She looked up at him, her eyes troubled. 'You must realise it wouldn't be right for me to agree to anything I don't feel comfortable with.'

Alfred nodded. 'Emma would scold me for raising the subject but I wanted to say how sorry I am. You'd be the making of that young man, even though, to give him his due, he's come a long way already.'

Grace sighed. 'You pay me a compliment, Mr Hicks. But I don't deserve it. Matthew feels things are about to change within the household. He may well be right but it's too soon to say and I need time to weigh up my situation, if indeed I'm faced with a choice regarding my own future.'

'The lad's more astute than I took him to be.' Alfred looked up at a crowd of starlings swirling overhead like a plume of smoke. He shook his head slowly. 'I agree with him that changes lie ahead. But for the time being, more than that I cannot say.'

'Here comes Emma,' said Grace. 'How much longer do you think we'll take to get there, Mr Hicks?'

'I reckon another half an hour should do it.'

'If you're both ready then, let's go and see the sea!' Grace took her seat in the front, wondering exactly how Mr Hicks's ideas of change compared with those of his nephew.

She enjoyed watching for landmarks as they drew closer to their destination. At last, she saw the chimneys of Admiral's Rest rising above the fields in the distance. Alfred slowed the vehicle ready to tackle the narrow, twisting lanes they must negotiate. Colourful wild flowers starred the hedgerows and narrow grass verges.

'You've done well, Mr Hicks.' As soon as Alfred drew up, Emma was gathering the picnic things.

'I didn't hang about and that's a fact.

Let me open your doors for you ladies.'

The three of them stood on the gravelled drive looking up at the lovely old house they all knew so well. Grace walked to the paved area before the front door, with key in hand ready to unlock the summer residence.

Alfred was already unloading their modest luggage. Emma followed Grace and stepped inside. She sniffed. 'Smells musty!'

'As you'd expect.' Alfred loomed behind her.

Grace wondered if she'd imagined it, or had he given a more than cordial look at Emma? She picked up a scattering of engraved calling cards from the floor. 'It looks as if the family will be welcoming all the usual suspects this summer.' She frowned as she read the details of the last one. 'Although this is a newcomer, by the looks of it. A Mister Harry Gresham.'

'Not another prospective suitor for Miss Rowena, surely?' Alfred was heading for the stairs. 'I'm taking these straight up to the top floor, ladies.'

Grace noted Emma frowning at her. 'I don't mean to pry, Emma, but this Mr Gresham gives Sea Breezes as his summer residence. His home is actually in New England.'

'So, he must be renting the house next door. Let's hope he doesn't sweep Miss Rowena off to America, although I can't see their lordships agreeing to that, can you, Grace?'

'They probably wouldn't appreciate a suitor who doesn't come from British stock. But I wouldn't dream of trying to guess Mr Gresham's pedigree.'

Emma chuckled. 'Maybe he has so much money, his ancestry — or lack of it — doesn't matter. Times are changing fast.'

'Not on my watch they aren't. And don't forget to run the water a while before you fill that kettle!' Alfred's deep voice floated down from the next floor.

Emma shook her head at Grace. 'Why do men always assume we know nothing at all?'

Matthew popped his head round the stillroom door and found the new maid up to her elbows in soap suds.

'I'm forever blowing bubbles,' he sang. 'Pretty bubbles in the air.'

Before he could warble another note, Polly piped up with the next two lines, her soprano voice sweet and clear. 'They fly so high, nearly reach the sky, then like my dreams they fade and die.'

Matthew stared at her, open-mouthed. 'Where did you learn to sing like that?'

'Like what? I can't help how I sounds.'

'I meant, how do you make the words seem so sad?'

'Because they are sad, that's how.' She went on washing up the luncheon crockery.

'Do you have dreams, Polly?'

The young maid sniggered. 'None that I'd tell you, Mr Hicks.'

'Call me Matt. My uncle is the only Mr Hicks round here.'

'I know that, but I don't want to put

a foot wrong and get chucked out.'

He walked up to her and touched her on the shoulder. Gently. 'You're doing well, Polly. I'll soon mark your card if I catch you doing something the wrong way, but somehow I don't think you will.'

Her face split into a grin. 'You're all right, you are, Matt.'

'Matthew, may I have a word please?'

He whirled round to find the daughter of the house smiling at him. Rowena, dressed in a mid-thigh-length blue skirt and jacket, stood in the doorway. She'd pulled a sapphire-blue velvet cloche hat on over her newly styled hair and Matt couldn't help but stare in open admiration. He only remembered to close his mouth when Polly's sharp elbow dug him in the ribs.

'I'm sorry, Miss Rowena. What can I do to help you?'

'Just a moment.' She peered around him. 'You must be Polly? I hope you'll be very happy with us.'

The young girl gave an awkward little

bob. 'Thank you, miss, I'm sure I shall be.'

Rowena turned her attention back to Matthew. 'I have a fancy to learn to drive. Do you think you could teach me?'

He swallowed hard. 'But you're a lady!'

Rowena rolled her big brown eyes at him. 'Ten out of ten for noticing. But what has that fact to do with anything?'

'Um . . . nothing. I'm sorry, Miss Rowena. You caught me by surprise, that's all. His lordship may prefer Mr Hicks to instruct you.'

Rowena made a face. 'I don't want to wait that long. Later today would be perfect. After I return from my luncheon engagement.'

'Do you require me to chauffeur you there, miss?' Matt tried to recover himself.

'No thanks, Matthew. Sir Redvers will be collecting me very soon.' She smiled at him. 'You might enjoy taking a look at his car. He drove me home in it last night though for the life of me I don't know what make it is. Anyway, I'll come and look for you promptly at four o'clock.' She turned around and crossed the kitchen, giving the cook a friendly wave on her way.

'Cripes,' said Polly, resuming her labours. 'Is she always like that?'

'Unfortunately yes.' Matt wondered what his uncle would say when he found out Miss Rowena had a mind to drive herself around London. This was a right old turn up for the book with no Uncle Alfred around to guide him through the predicament. Never mind about his uncle — did his lordship know about Miss Rowena's strange request? And what was all the hurry about?

'Looks to me,' said Polly, 'like Miss Rowena's taken a real shine to you.'

'What nonsense you talk. I told you what she's like.'

He hardly noticed the wistful expression on the new maid's face as she held a dripping egg whisk up to inspect for cleanliness. He knew there was only one person he could consult and he was instructed to collect that person from his offices at noon and drive him to his club for luncheon. If his lordship knew all about Miss Rowena's sudden new interest in motoring, Matt would gladly do his best to instruct her in the art of driving. Maybe it was all for the best that Uncle Alfred was out of town. He'd been strict enough when teaching his own nephew to drive. He might well find sitting in the passenger seat beside a woman motorist a bridge too far to cross.

★   ★   ★

The church clock across the square chimed four times as Matthew, waiting beside the Daimler, saw Miss Rowena come through the back door and hurry across the courtyard. She'd changed from her pretty blue picnic outfit into a long-sleeved white blouse topped with a black waistcoat, worn over velvet knickerbockers. Her hair was swathed in a white chiffon scarf and she was pulling on a pair of black leather driving gloves. They alone probably cost more than his week's wages, Matthew mused.

'Ready?' His pupil stood, hands on hips. 'Where do I start?'

Matthew offered up a prayer that he might remember all he'd been taught and would relay it to his enthusiastic pupil with all the confidence he could muster.

He opened the passenger door. 'If you sit here, Miss Rowena, you can watch carefully while I show you how we gets going.'

She climbed in and settled herself. He sat behind the wheel and went through the different controls with her, noting with surprise the extreme concentration she displayed. After he'd driven around the courtyard several times, braking and stopping on the way, he asked her to change places.

Rowena peered over the driving wheel and made a face. Matt hid a smile and reached into the back for a cushion. 'You'll find it more comfortable and easier to see if you sit on this, miss.'

'Ah, that's better.' She beamed at him. 'But you must call me Rowena while you're teaching me. It's too silly otherwise.'

'That'll be difficult for me, miss.'

He watched her pout.

'Please try, Matthew.'

'I'll do my level best to remember, miss . . . Rowena. Now, think about what I said to you and start the engine, please.' He gulped. 'Gently, is what I meant to say.'

Matt held his breath as his pupil engaged first gear. Briefly he closed his eyes as he felt the car move forward, jerking enough for him to open his eyes and yell but suddenly the Daimler slid forward again, smoothly this time.

'We're heading for the gateway.' He sucked in his breath. 'Miss? I mean, Rowena? I wasn't planning on showing you how to reverse yet!'

She didn't turn her head to look at him. 'I might as well have a proper go, don't you think? Going round in circles is pointless.'

'Blimey.' Stunned, Matthew peered through the windscreen as they sailed serenely out of the courtyard and down the side road.

'Where do you want me to go?'

'Next left turn would be good. I don't want us ending up at Oxford bleedin' Circus — oh, sorry, miss. Here we go . . .'

Rowena turned the wheel and the car eased around the corner of the pavement.

'Now change gear again.' Matt felt his shoulders relax. But he stiffened, hearing the engine's mangled shriek of protest. 'Remember what I showed you?'

'Sorry, Matt. I'll do it right this time, you wait and see.'

They were progressing at a sedate pace and as Matthew sneaked a glance at his pupil, he reckoned she looked as though she'd been driving for years. If they could only get home in one piece, he'd be forever grateful and with any luck he'd find Lord Carmichael would need him to remain on standby for the rest of the day.

'Watch out!' Matt yelled as an urchin shot across the road in front of the vehicle. The lad thumbed his nose at them as Rowena applied the brakes and brought the Daimler to a surprisingly smooth standstill.

Matt wound down his window. 'You had a lucky escape, nipper. Take care in future, ay?'

'Rather you than me, mister!' The boy yelled and ran away, sniggering.

Rowena burst out laughing. 'Poor Matt. You know, I'm rather enjoying this. Hold on to your hat now!'

It didn't quite come to that, but Matt felt much relieved when at last they were home again and Mrs Potter took in a tea tray to Rowena and returned to pour him a cup of hot, sweet tea from her bottomless pot.

She sat down at the head of the

kitchen table. 'You wouldn't get me in one of those contraptions for all the tea in China.'

Matt knew Mrs Potter always insisted upon travelling to the coast by train when she worked her usual four weeks at Admiral's Rest. He inhaled the delicious aroma of roasting beef and picked a piece of homemade shortbread from the square tin with the Union Jack emblem on its lid. 'You've saved my life, Mrs P, and that's a fact.' He crunched the biscuit.

'How long will it take you to teach her? I still can't believe his lordship agreed to these shenanigans.'

Matt swallowed a mouthful of tea. 'I wouldn't have taken it upon myself to give miss Rowena lessons without her pa's approval, now, would I?'

'I s'pose not. For the life of me, I don't understand why she can't wait for Mr Hicks to come back.'

'Miss Rowena likes to get up and go. She takes every opportunity she can. I envy her in some ways.'

The cook sniffed and stirred her tea so the spoon clinked against the china cup. 'That's not like you. I thought you were pretty happy with your lot.' She put one hand to her mouth. 'I'm sorry, Matthew. I should've thought before saying that.'

'Don't apologise. Grace has made her feelings perfectly plain. It's pointless me trying to keep it secret.'

'Sometimes I don't understand young people. Don't know they're born, some of 'em. Present company not included of course.'

'I count myself as flattered.' Matt leaned forward, lacing his fingers around his teacup.

'Then there's some of us who don't realise what's plain as the nose upon their face.'

'What's that? Who are you talking about, Mrs P?'

But the cook pursed her lips and looked mysterious. 'It's not for me to say. Sometimes the onlooker sees most of the game.'

Matt frowned. For the life of him he couldn't think what Mrs Potter meant and he decided to leave the matter rest.

'What's young Polly up to?' He leaned back in his chair and looked up at the kitchen clock. He had plenty of time before he picked up his employer from his club. Matt never ceased to be amazed at the amount of business Lord Carmichael conducted at his club in Pall Mall or on the golf course.

Why was Mrs Potter trying to hide her mirth from him? What had he said this time? It was Matthew's humble opinion that the female of the human race must definitely belong to a different species.

4

In the kitchen of the house perched high above the sea, Alfred Hicks sat at the table. He'd spread a layer of newspaper before beginning on the laborious task of polishing the silver cutlery and candlesticks he'd lovingly packed up the previous September for storage in the London residence. Here they were again, being shined up ready for family meals and the more elaborate dinners arranged when her ladyship entertained guests from London as well as from the local gentry.

Emma walked in, her face flushed and with a strand of hair escaping from the green cotton scarf she'd wrapped around her head.

Alfred looked up at her and smiled. 'Hot work?'

'I'll say. But we're making good progress upstairs. There's a bottle of homemade lemonade standing on the marble shelf. Shall I call Grace so we can all take a break?'

Alfred sat up straight and put down his polishing cloth. 'In a minute. Emma, it's high time you and me had ourselves a little chat.'

She pulled her scarf off and shook her coppery curls free to fall around her face. 'I . . . you and me . . . we go back a long way, Alfred.'

He pulled off his chamois leather gloves and stood up, his face serious. 'We also have much in common. Would you say yes if I asked you to take an evening stroll after supper?'

She hesitated. 'Someone should stay in and I don't want to leave Grace here on her own.'

'She might enjoy it. You know how she likes to explore the library if she only gets the chance. Without Miss Rowena racketing round, she'll probably jump at the opportunity.'

'Shall I ask her then?'

Alfred's face lit up but he had no

time to answer before Grace entered the kitchen. 'Shall you ask who what?' Her eyes shone with laughter.

'Mr Hicks has invited me to take a stroll with him later. Would that be all right with you?'

'Goodness me, yes indeed. About time too!' Grace grinned at Alfred. 'I'm happy to potter about the garden and see what plants have come through as long as I can go down to the beach tomorrow for a while. The weather's set fair, don't you agree, Mr Hicks?'

'I should say so, Grace. Now, how about that cold drink, Emma?'

Grace knew the three of them made a conscientious trio when it came to the job in hand. The house having been shut up all winter required hours of airing, but it meant there were no rough chores to do, although Emma insisted that she'd scrub the kitchen floor on their last morning. This request from Alfred to walk out with Emma made her feel very happy indeed. She'd felt for a long time that the two of them belonged together as a couple and now it seemed she could be proved right.

How strange to think that Emma and Alfred might soon be facing an important decision, while back in London Rowena appeared to be on the verge of a new phase in her young life. And what of herself, she wondered as she sipped cool, tangy lemonade and nibbled a light-as-a-feather fairy cake. Alfred Hicks was consulting the local newspaper they'd picked up on the way and smiling with pleasure as he announced there'd be a low tide that evening, just the thing for his and Emma's stroll on the seashore.

'That'll be almost as good tomorrow, then? For Grace to take a walk, I mean.'

Grace, hearing Emma mention her name, tried to concentrate on the moment. She'd had decisions made on her behalf for so many years now, the prospect of breaking out of her long-established routine gave her a tremulous feeling, like butterflies dancing the polka in her stomach. How silly of her!

'There's no reason why the pair of you can't go to the beach together tomorrow,' said Alfred. 'But you know I think it's best one of us stays around when we're down here without the family. I wouldn't want his lordship to ring and find I'd skived off.'

'We'll see.' Grace shot a mischievous glance at her friend. 'You might prefer to take the opportunity to spend time alone together. That's something you're not going to find easy when we're back in town again.'

'Grace! That's a little presumptuous, don't you think?' This time, Grace thought the fetching pink of Emma's cheeks owed nothing to physical exertion.

Alfred cleared his throat. 'But what Grace says is true nonetheless.' He drained his glass. 'Now, I must get on. I want to have this lot finished and the table cleared by six o'clock. Will that suit, ladies?'

★ ★ ★

He was true to his word and after they'd eaten cold meat and new potatoes with fresh vegetables Polly had been sent to buy from the nearest market early that morning, Grace decided his patience should be rewarded.

'Off you go, you two,' she said when all the plates were cleared.

'But what about the washing-up?'

'This is nothing compared to what there is at Seymour House. No arguments, Emma. Or you, Mr Hicks.'

'You could call me Alfred, you know, Grace.'

'Thank you. Perhaps, while we're down here, but not once we're back in London.' She smiled at him. 'Now off you go, before I change my mind.'

'I must powder my nose. I shan't be a minute.' Emma rushed from the room, skirt whirling around her legs.

Alfred gazed after her. 'Do you think she'll say yes?'

Grace surprised both him and herself by flinging her arms around him. 'I never guessed you were such a romantic, Alfred.'

She stood back and watched him straighten his tie. 'Even if it has taken you years to get around to a proposal.'

He chuckled and headed outside through the back door. Soon Emma was back and once the pair had left, Grace, finding the sudden silence strange but oddly welcome, washed and rinsed the supper things and dried them with a pristine linen cloth.

The evening sunshine was too tempting to resist so she changed into a pair of walking shoes and headed out to the kitchen garden. Lord Carmichael employed a local man to keep an eye on the not-so-small piece of land upon which Admiral's Rest stood.

She wandered along the rows, foreseeing the prospect of tender runner beans and luscious Dorset strawberries in the coming weeks. Alfred would be kept busy. Or would it be Matt driving the family down here before very much longer? What would Rowena say when her mother decided to spend a long weekend at the coast? Would she insist on inviting Sir

Redvers to join the assembled company, knowing this landmark first weekend away was normally a family only occasion, with the exception of Grace?

Later on, after the flood of important social engagements had dried up and August loomed, Lord Carmichael would spend half the week in town and half at Admiral's Rest. Grace hoped life wouldn't be too difficult for Emma and Alfred in the throes of their fledging romance and, as intimated by Alfred, their forthcoming betrothal.

'I hope it's not a case of becoming star-crossed lovers.' Grace muttered the words aloud, almost without realising, as she strolled along the high fence dividing the kitchen garden from the grounds of Sea Breezes.

'*Romeo and Juliet* by the great William Shakespeare? That line in the prologue sure blew the plot for me.'

Grace froze. The unseen speaker must be standing directly behind the barrier separating her from none other than the current tenant of Sea Breezes.

Unless, of course, the voice belonged to someone employed to tend the garden. This, she decided, was unlikely, given the unmistakable transatlantic tinge to the words spoken in a melodious baritone.

'Good evening,' she called. 'I apologise for speaking out loud.'

'And I apologise for eavesdropping upon your conversation with yourself, ma'am.'

Grace's lips twitched. She admired his sense of humour. 'I don't make a habit of talking to myself.'

'Me neither. But you know what? With my solitary lifestyle down here, I'm kind of growing accustomed to hearing myself do that very thing.'

She tried to picture the name she'd skimmed over on the calling card. Larry? No, but now she had it.

'Would you by any chance be Mr Harry Gresham?'

'I would indeed be Harry Gresham, especially if it means you'll talk to him instead of to yourself. How do you do, Miss . . . ?

'I'm Grace . . . Grace Maxwell.' She pressed both hands to her lips but it was too late. What on earth could have possessed her to blurt out the name she knew belonged to the Edinburgh family for whom her late mother worked before she and Grace's father moved to London?

'Maxwell, hmmm? My, that's interesting. And are Lord and Lady Carmichael in residence, Miss Grace Maxwell? The word in the village was that Admiral's Rest would be opened up very soon.'

She managed to reply, 'I can imagine the jungle drums have been beating. The house is being prepared over the next couple of days. So far there's just me, our chauffeur-cum-butler and our housekeeper in residence.'

'I hope you didn't think it presumptuous of me to leave my calling card. It seemed like the neighbourly thing to do.'

'Lady Cressida will be delighted, I'm sure.'

'It sounds like her ladyship isn't your mama, Grace?'

'Correct.'

'Forgive me,' said Harry. 'My mother warned me not to be too inquisitive. You British are far more reserved than we Americans, I guess.'

'Oh, we do our share of wondering and presuming.'

'And what are you wondering now, Grace? I do hope I may call you by your very lovely name.'

She felt her heartbeat quicken. This man was flirting with her! Generally that only happened among the tradesmen she dealt with and took the form of entirely friendly and harmless banter. Rowena of course was accustomed to receiving compliments and juggling the amorous young men who became interested in her, or sometimes latched onto her eligible status, as she frequently grumbled to Grace.

'Are you still there, behind this annoying fence?'

'Yes, I'm still here.'

'Are you as pretty as your voice suggests?'

'Beauty is in the eye of the beholder, Mr Gresham.'

'Touché, ma'am. Will I be permitted to call upon you, or does her ladyship have to be consulted in the matter? You'll have to help me, Grace. British etiquette's double Dutch to me.'

He sounded lovely. He was obviously becoming disenchanted with his own company. Grace closed her eyes and made a decision. 'I can't invite you indoors. That wouldn't be proper.' She left the meaning behind the remark for him to take in.

Sharp as a tack, he didn't hesitate. 'Then will you walk around to your front gates and allow me to talk to you while I stand on the highway?'

Grace thanked her lucky stars Emma had suggested they all change from their work clothes to eat the evening meal. She wore a floral-patterned blue-and-white cotton dress with a fluffy white Angora cardigan draped around her shoulders. As she walked around the side of the house towards the gates, carefully closed by Alfred earlier when he took Emma for an evening stroll, she wondered whether she'd totally lost her reason. This wasn't the way she'd behave in London. How awful it would be if Harry Gresham decided she must be fast, as she knew from the gossip Rowena provided that it appeared many young women were. She'd once heard Lady Cressida describe some poor unfortunate girl as nothing but a hussy and shivered at the thought of what the American gentleman might make of her eagerness to meet him with only the click of a latch separating them.

But when Harry appeared and smiled at her, grasping the top rail of the gate to watch her approach, Grace felt all her fears melt away. This young man meant no harm. For all his assured comments spoken from behind the wooden fence, he had an air of shyness about him, as if he too couldn't believe this impromptu meeting was happening out of the blue. The colour of his hair reminded her of shiny conkers and he wore horn-rimmed spectacles through which his dark brown eyes sparkled with humour.

'Grace. Please don't be afraid of me. I'm so very pleased to meet you face to face.' He offered his hand.

'Good evening, Mr Gresham.' She held out her hand and noted his gentle yet firm, warm handshake.

'Ah, now that's a mite unfair of you. I get to call you Grace, so can you not call me Harry?'

'All right. I'm delighted to make your acquaintance, Harry.'

'Pardon me, but I have to ask: are you one of the star-crossed lovers I heard you mention?' He was still holding on to her hand.

She burst out laughing. 'Goodness, no. I was weighing up a certain situation involving two people I'm fond of but which has nothing to do with me.'

'Well, that's a relief.'

She looked down at their clasped hands, then looked up into his eyes, and for the very first time in her life fell head over heels in love.

★　★　★

Next day while Grace and Emma washed up the luncheon things and dried and put them away, Alfred was tinkering with a mantelpiece clock.

'I reckon I can make this old fellow tick again,' he said. 'If not, I shall take it back with us and leave it with the clockmaker.'

Emma walked over to him and put her hand on his shoulder. 'Oh, please don't speak of going back, Alfred. I'm so enjoying being here with both of you, putting everything in order.'

Grace finished emptying away the washing-up water and turned to face the two people who she knew cared so deeply about her welfare. She knew she must confess that Harry Gresham had asked her to take a stroll with him that evening. Emma and Alfred listened in silence as she described the chance meeting and the resulting invitation.

'So I thought there'd be no harm in taking a walk with him. You two can have the place to yourselves for an hour or so. You must have so much to talk about.'

Grace watched Emma and Alfred exchange glances. Emma had a slightly puzzled expression on her face but Alfred was frowning.

'We can't forbid you to go out with this young man,' he said. 'But I question whether he's a suitable escort for you.'

'Because he's American? Or because he's a toff?'

'Oh my lovely girl!' Emma's outburst caught Grace by surprise, as did the tears in the eyes of the woman who'd occupied the role of second mother to her all these years.

'It's only a stroll,' said Grace. 'He's feeling a bit lonely, that's all.' She kept her tone light-hearted.

'What was he thinking of, renting a place all on his own, then?' Alfred sniffed. 'I hope he's not leading you on, because he'll have me to reckon with if he's that sort of chap.'

'Grace is too level-headed to swallow any old nonsense,' said Emma. 'I'm all for her having a bit of fun for herself for once instead of running around after Miss Rowena.'

'An American might have certain ideas, is all I'm saying.' Alfred was obviously embarrassed. 'How can he possibly understand our ways and our notions of class?'

'Grace is as well-bred as any other young woman Mr Gresham is likely to come across,' Emma said sharply. 'Better than many, I'd say.'

Grace watched the look of puzzlement upon Alfred's face. What was going on here? She'd never have described herself as well-bred. Didn't that involve one's bloodline? It concerned ancestry and not merely years of learning correct table manners and how to behave at the theatre and other public places, along with Rowena. Grace knew how to act like a lady while knowing full well all the tradesmen and the other employees regarded her as an orphaned girl who'd been lucky enough to gain the guardianship and support of Lord and Lady Carmichael.

'As I say, it's none of our business and I'm sure you know what you're doing, Grace.' Alfred sat back, a look of triumph on his face. 'There! I knew I could bring this clock back to life. It's ticking sweet as a nut.'

They all three returned to their chores and the afternoon flew by for Grace as she and Emma concentrated upon making up the numerous beds with freshly-laundered linen and tucking lavender bags inside snowy pillow cases. Alfred had arranged for a chimney sweep to visit early that morning and afterwards the chauffeur-cum-butler and jack-of-all-trades, as he described himself, cleaned all the grates and shined up the fire-irons and brass fenders before replacing candlesticks and clocks on the mantelpieces around the property.

After a tasty cottage pie supper, Grace hurried up to the top floor to prepare for her rendezvous with Harry Gresham. It didn't in the least bother her that she had to occupy a servant's room, leaving any available rooms on the second floor in readiness for guest occupancy. Again, she wondered which of the London domestic staff would be travelling down for the first weekend in Dorset. There'd be one to cook, one to do the driving and help out with the garden, and probably Grace herself helping out where she could, unless the new girl proved so useful that she could take a turn too.

When Grace came downstairs wearing the red-and-white two-piece she'd worn for her cinema outing with Matt, she found Emma and Alfred unashamedly holding hands across the kitchen table.

'Don't mind me.' Grace smiled at them and performed a little twirl. 'Do I look all right?'

'Very nice,' said Alfred.

'You look beautiful, my dear.' But Emma pulled her hand away from Alfred's and reached into her pocket for a handkerchief.

'Emma? What's wrong?' Grace was at her side in moments.

'It . . . it's nothing.' She sniffed and dabbed at her cheeks. 'You go and enjoy yourself.'

'It might be because Emma and I have something to tell you,' Alfred chimed in. 'You ladies can be a little emotional sometimes.'

'Alfred has asked me to marry him and I've said yes.' Emma blew her nose noisily.

'That's wonderful.' Grace gave Emma a hug. 'Nothing to cry about.'

Alfred rose to shake her hand but Grace placed a kiss on his cheek, laughing at the surprised expression on his face. She wouldn't have made these affectionate gestures back in London.

'Am I the first to know?'

'You are, Grace, and I'd be obliged if you'd keep our engagement secret until I've had a chance to inform his lordship regarding our future plans.'

Grace looked from one to the other of them. The doorbell clanged, making her jump. Temporarily she'd forgotten all about Harry Gresham.

'I'll go and let him in,' said Alfred.

Alone with Emma, Grace seized her chance. 'I couldn't help noticing how you took one look at me and the tears welled up at once, Emma. Why was that? You're obviously starry-eyed over Alfred, as well you should be.'

But Emma wouldn't meet her eyes. 'You . . . you looked so like . . . your dear mother when you walked in,' she said. 'I was wishing she could be here with us, that's all.'

Grace heard the rumble of voices from the hall and hoped Alfred wasn't treating Harry to a potted version of the British class system. But something about

111

Emma's reaction to her appearance didn't seem right and she determined to discover what really had triggered the sudden rush of emotion.

'I thought I was supposed to take after my father's mother,' she said. 'There are no photographs of my grandma for me to look at but certainly the ones of my own mother bear no resemblance to me whatsoever. I'm much darker and taller than she was.'

'These things happen across the generations,' said Emma. 'Now, off you go and enjoy your walk. I wonder if it's in order to invite Mr Gresham in for a cup of coffee when he brings you home.'

'Goodness. I don't know. I suppose it depends upon what Alfred thinks.'

'There's two of us and one of him, don't forget. But see how you get on first. We'll be here, waiting for you. After all, Mr Gresham is a neighbour for the summer and may well be entertained here in future.'

But as Grace walked into the hallway,

where Harry and Alfred were already talking about cars, she told herself Lady Cressida would surely disapprove of Grace acting as hostess on her behalf, albeit on a temporary basis. Some things were sacred, despite Rowena's frequent protestations to her mother about how they were living in the year 1925 and not 1875 when her ladyship had been born.

Grace and Harry walked down the driveway and through the gates before he offered her his arm.

'I wasn't sure if Alfred and Emma would consider me too forward by presuming you might like to take my arm after such a brief acquaintance-ship.'

Grace laughed. 'You worry too much. It's very pleasant to walk arm in arm on such a lovely evening.'

He nodded, shooting her a quick glance, the admiration in his gaze sending shivers down her spine. 'I know there's a bench just by the cliff path,' he said. 'Are you happy to go down to the shore first and maybe take a seat and get our breath back after our climb back up again?'

'That sounds fine to me.' She pointed to a gateway to their left. 'That house belongs to a very delightful family. Have you met the Ashmores yet?'

'No. According to my new friend the fishmonger, the folks who live in that mansion are out of the country and won't be back for another couple of weeks. See how well-informed I am?'

'I'm impressed. Well, when you do meet them you'll find them very charming. They have a daughter called Tulip. She's a feminist and much admired by Rowena.'

'Ha! And by you, I guess?'

'I have a sneaking admiration for Miss Ashmore, yes. I doubt she'd approve of my role in life though.'

'Then more fool her.'

'They also have a son, George, who's probably around your age. He spends most of August with them every year.'

'Is he the one that's sweet on you? If

so, I dislike him already, although I have to admire his good taste.'

Grace stopped walking. 'Whatever makes you think George Ashmore might pay attention to me?'

'The esteemed Mr Hicks told me you had a suitor, that's all. I guess he was marking my card, Grace. It took the wind out of my sails but I might've guessed such a beautiful girl as you would have dozens of admirers.'

'Hardly that. Well, one maybe.' She thought of the awkward situation around Matt and couldn't help but feel guilty.

'One! Is this an example of the famous British sense of humour? I came across it on my visit to Scotland some years ago. In fact, I have a friend who shares your surname. Might he be a relation I wonder? There's a distinct similarity about the two of you, now I come to think of it.'

'Oh, I very much doubt that.' Her stomach lurched. Why, oh why, had she been so stupid as to give Harry a false name, especially one with aristocratic connections?

'Hell's teeth! Pardon me, Grace, but it's all becoming clear now. My friend Alexander's mother is a beautiful dark-haired lady like yourself. She's a lot older than you of course, but there's a photograph of Lady Iona as a debutante on the living-room wall in Glenbarrie House, and now I know why I kind of felt like you and I had met before. You're a younger version of her.'

5

Glenbarrie House! The name sounded so familiar. Could she perhaps, back in her childhood, while playing or studying with Rowena, have heard her mother mention that name to Emma? Oh dear lord, what was this man going to think of her? She needed to explain her status before he fabricated some extraordinary family history for her that patently did not exist.

'Harry, I think I need to make something clear to you.'

'I'm listening.' With his free hand he squeezed her fingers resting so lightly on his arm.

'I'm afraid you might have misunderstood my presence here.'

'Well, you're obviously not a servant. I wondered whether you might be here to supervise the house preparation.'

'I'm here to help with it in fact. Lord

and Lady Carmichael are officially my employers, although they have acted as my guardians ever since I lost my mother when I was just thirteen years of age.'

It was Harry's turn to stop walking now. 'I am so very sorry to hear of your loss, Grace. So you have no connection to my Scottish friends? Yet how is it you sound so . . . so deliciously aristocratic? You're surely not asking me to believe you're carrying out the duties of a servant? Not that I don't respect maids and cooks and governesses, don't get me wrong!'

'I act as companion and lady's maid to the daughter of the house. But my late mother was employed at Seymour House, the London residence. That's how she became so friendly with Emma, who became my second mother in many ways. I've been educated with the Honourable Rowena Carmichael and we get on very well, but my social life is virtually non-existent, Harry. The suitor I mentioned just now is in fact the nephew of Alfred Hicks and he's a hardworking, trustworthy young man but . . . ' She faltered. 'I knew my feelings for him weren't the same as his for me so I turned him down as gently as I could. He wasn't afraid to accuse me of looking to better myself by marrying out of my class.'

'I don't know what to say.'

'We can go back to the house if you wish. I'll understand if you feel cheated in some way.'

'Cheated! Holy mackerel, Grace, right now I feel like the luckiest guy on the planet. May I kiss you? Please say yes.'

She couldn't believe what she heard.

He took both her hands in his. 'Believe me, I'd be asking you that question if you were a duchess or a kitchen maid. I'd probably be nervous around you if you were a duchess, although to tell the truth I couldn't care less about all that class stuff. It's what you are, not who you are! Believe me. Trust me, Grace, please.'

The tenderness in his eyes drew her

closer to him. She leaned towards him and kissed him lightly on his cheek. He took her in his arms and held her tenderly for a few moments before he tipped her chin upwards and kissed her gently on her mouth. She closed her eyes and felt his lips upon hers a second time. This time the kiss was sweeter and more significant.

'We should continue walking,' Harry whispered at last. 'You must think me very forward.'

'Different,' she said, taking his arm again. 'But in a good way.'

'Well, that's a relief,' he said. 'I didn't mean to rush you but I'd sure like to see you again.'

'We've hardly got to know one another. I might not share your interests. I know nothing about baseball, for instance.'

He chuckled. 'Nor do I. My father will never get over the fact. And we both know something of Shakespeare.'

'I prefer Dickens.'

'My mom has every one of that esteemed author's books. I have a feeling she'd be better conversing about Oliver, Nancy and Bill Sykes than I would.'

'What do you like, Harry?'

'Apart from you?'

'Behave!'

'OK. I like fossils. I'm crazy about them and always have been. That's why I'm here in Dorset, renting a house all on my own. And I like tennis and jazz and food and movies and, oh heck, lots of things. Not dancing — I have two left feet.'

'I've never had dancing lessons, but I play tennis with Rowena sometimes.'

'Will I get to meet this girl some day?'

'I think it's highly likely. But I won't be in evidence if you attend a dinner party here. If she hasn't invited an escort, you'll be paired with her or some other suitable young woman. Maybe Tulip Ashmore from the house I pointed out.'

'No way. I shall refuse point-blank to attend unless I have you at my side.' He helped her down onto the shingle, eyes blazing with determination. 'Anyway, feminists frighten the daylights out of me.'

'Oh, Harry. You know what I'm about to say?'

'I'm willing to listen but I may not agree.'

'I wouldn't wish you to become one of a pair of star-crossed lovers. I'm afraid I'm firmly out of bounds for you.'

'Grace, my lovely Grace, don't you dare say such a thing. I couldn't care less about dinner parties. I only want to meet Rowena because you seem fond of her, is all. Why are Lord and Lady Carmichael treating you in such a strange manner?'

'They're treating me very well, considering my social status.' She tried to keep her voice calm but even so, couldn't avoid the tremor.

He pulled her close to him. She leaned her head against him and he stroked her hair into place after the playful breeze lifted it away from her face.

'So do you have any kin who care about you? Any aunts or uncles or cousins who are around your age? Do you have your mother's photograph album and stuff like that?'

'Nothing except a beautiful silver locket she left me. You can imagine how much I treasure it.'

He looked thoughtful. 'Hmm. You're a bit of a mystery woman. My mind's working overtime here.'

'I can't think why. I'm very ordinary and I shouldn't have played along when you called out to me in the garden. We should enjoy the rest of the evening and leave things how they are.'

'You think I'm about to let you go now I've found you? You think my mother hasn't thrown suitable young women in my path over the last five years or so? Not one of those girls has ever made me feel like I do over you, Grace Walker.'

She moved away from him, feeling the tears spring to her eyes.

He pulled her close again and stroked

her cheek. 'We can sort this. I can visit you in London. We'll meet in secret if that's what it takes. I'm kind of getting a hunch about certain matters and I need to talk to people, apart from the boffins I have to hook up with to discuss my geological assignment.'

'So you teach?'

'I'm a college professor.'

'Oh my word.' Grace swallowed hard. Of course . . . hadn't she read his business card? Her eye had picked up the name of a single man but hadn't registered his professorial title. She'd forgotten the name as soon as she replaced the card at the bottom of the pile on the hall table. But from the moment they'd begun conversing through the garden fence she'd become attracted to him and obviously lost all the sense she'd been born with. She and Harry moved in very different worlds. There could be no future in their relationship, such as it was. And at that moment, despite his pledge to see her again, she felt plunged into a well of despair, something she'd never imagined feeling when she set off for the coast with Emma and Alfred the day before. If this was love, it could only bring heartache.

But when he asked her if she'd allow him to drive her to a little place up the coast the following evening for supper, she heard herself accepting the invitation.

She asked him to tell her something about the fossils about which she knew very little and saw his face light up. She could tell how passionate he was about his subject but she could see how young women like those among Rowena's crowd would prefer someone who'd take them dancing rather than digging up the past.

★ ★ ★

'So you decided not to invite the young gentleman in?' Emma looked up from the tray cloth she was embroidering as Grace walked into the kitchen after her walk.

'I thought it best not to.' Grace went over to the sink and filled a tumbler with water. 'Where's Alfred?'

'Speaking on the telephone to his lordship.'

'Is everything all right back in London?' Grace sipped the water.

'We'll find out very soon, I expect.' Emma pushed aside tumbled skeins of jewel-coloured embroidery silks and put down her sewing. 'Are you all right, my dear?'

'I'm fine. Oh, Emma, why does life have to be so difficult?'

'Mr Gresham hasn't upset you, has he? Oh dear, maybe I shouldn't have encouraged you to accept his invitation.'

'He hasn't upset me in the least. Harry Gresham is . . . he's kind and funny and lovely and . . . '

Emma nodded. 'You don't need to say any more. I can tell from your face what's going on. Does he feel the same, do you think?'

'He has invited me out to supper

tomorrow evening, but it doesn't matter if he really means it or not. In my stupidity I led him on. He assumed I was someone better than I am, until I decided things were getting out of hand and confessed.'

'Someone better? There's no one better than you, Grace. In what way were things getting out of hand?'

Grace told Emma how she and Harry Gresham had got on so well — too well in fact, given that they'd exchanged kisses. She also said that was the kind of thing Rowena did, and how she realised flirting and enjoying stolen kisses weren't her style, and to make matters worse she'd told Harry her name was Grace Maxwell and not Grace Walker. The words tumbled out in a torrent until Grace sank down in the chair opposite Emma and put her head in her hands.

But Emma didn't rush to comfort her. 'I can't believe you told him your name was Grace Maxwell. Whatever made you say such a thing?'

'I don't know!' Grace wailed. 'I was

carried away. Sometimes I get so sick and tired of always being the one to stay home while Rowena has all the attention and all the fun. I'm sorry, Emma. I know I have so much to be thankful for. Please ignore me. I'll just have to keep well out of the way if Harry Gresham comes to dinner and I happen to be down here.'

Grace thought of Matt again. He was the only other young man who'd expressed interest in her, and what had she done — ? Turned him down, that's what. She couldn't forget how he'd accused her of thinking herself too good for him. That hadn't been the reason at all, whatever Matt might think.

Now a second young man, although older and more sophisticated than Matthew, had come along; and she'd allowed him to flirt with her and ended up getting herself into deeper water than she ever intended. What was more, she'd lost her heart to the handsome young American — and much good it would do her, because this was a man she knew was very different from her. So not only would she now be avoiding Matthew Hicks, but she'd be living in fear of seeing Harry Gresham again, even though it was the one thing she wanted most in the world to happen.

She was so caught up in her own dilemma that she didn't notice Emma's silence.

'The odd thing was that Harry told me when he first saw me he thought I seemed familiar,' said Grace. 'He's friendly with the Maxwell family who live in Edinburgh. Obviously they're top-drawer, because he spoke of Lady Maxwell being a dark-haired beauty. I tried to draw him away from the subject because I was embarrassed about telling him a lie. I know my parents worked for a family of that name but if I look anything like the Lady Maxwell that Harry knows, that can only be down to a strange coincidence.'

Emma was staring at the satin stitch she'd been working on. Her usually serene expression was now more like a stormy sea and she opened her mouth and closed it again as though about to say something but had thought better of it.

'Emma?'

But Emma shook her head and her face, far from being pale, now flooded with colour.

In fact, thought Grace, both Emma and Harry had said some very puzzling things to her recently. That remark about the past coming back to haunt drifted into her mind. Emma had rushed from the room on that occasion and Grace hadn't questioned her as to what she meant. Now it was as though the world she'd known, the one she knew her way around, had been turned topsy-turvy without her noticing. And Emma was looking ashen again. In fact her face had turned as pale as the slender ivory candles kept in wooden holders on the table for fear of a power cut. Her fine complexion, swift to react to temperature changes or emotion, always gave her away, she often complained.

Grace, having had an awful thought, was agonising over the distinct possibility that by meeting Harry Gresham, she might have uncovered some dreadful secret about her parents and why they'd moved from the Scottish capital to London. What if they'd been caught stealing from the family? Had they fled the Maxwell household for London and forged a reference in order to obtain positions at Seymour House?

'I never dreamed something like this could happen,' whispered Emma. 'All I wanted was for you to have a little harmless enjoyment. I can't stop you seeing this young man again but please, please try to divert him from asking too many questions. Say you know nothing about the Maxwells.'

'But I don't, do I? Emma, what is all this about? Why can't you explain why you're so upset?'

But Emma shook her head and pursed her lips. 'I can't say. Not yet. Please believe me and . . . and go out one last time with Mr Gresham if that's what you wish, but remember we'll be back in London soon with everything back to normal.'

Grace stared at her. Emma hadn't spelt it out that Grace mustn't expect her position to be elevated merely because the American had taken a fancy to her, but it was obvious this was what she meant. Her suspicions about some murky episode involving her parents during their time in Edinburgh must be accurate. She felt sick at the thought of such awfulness, but her anguish was interrupted as Alfred came into the room, wearing a very pensive expression upon his face.

'Well, you could knock me down with a feather,' he said as he glanced at Emma. 'What's up?' He turned his attention to Grace. 'You two look as though you've seen a ghost apiece.'

'We're fine,' said Grace quickly. 'I'm afraid I've been boring Emma, telling her about Mr Gresham's fascination for fossils.'

Alfred laughed. 'Enough to turn

anyone pale. Though he seems a very polite gentleman. He was admiring the Daimler and telling me he's borrowed a Bugatti motorcar from his uncle in London.'

'Mr Gresham's invited Grace to have supper with him tomorrow evening.'

'That'll be our last night here,' said Alfred.

'Is that what his lordship rang to tell you?' Grace knew their stay at the coast was open-ended, pending how well the three of them got on with their preparations.

'It was. I told him I was confident we'd be finished by tomorrow afternoon but I'd prefer to set off early the following morning rather than travel when we'd all probably be very tired. Be prepared for all systems go when we return though.'

Grace felt weak with relief. Emma might feel Harry Gresham posed some kind of threat, but the thought of even a few more hours in his company filled her with joy. She'd deal with the situation as best she could and of course, once back in London, it would be pointless to pine after him. He'd be miles away, focused on his project, and she'd be kept busy with whatever Alfred Hicks was about to say to them. He had that look on his face that heralded important news. Whatever troubled Emma would have to wait for now, but Grace knew she'd remain tormented by doubts over the character of the only blood relatives she possessed in the world.

'What did you mean about all systems go?' Emma asked.

'Lady C has decided she wants to throw a party. Reading between the lines, I'd say she wants to show off this new beau of Miss Rowena's before the London season gets in full swing.' He turned to Grace. 'Did you know about the driving lessons? Matthew's been teaching Miss Rowena, according to his lordship.'

'Sometimes even I have a job to keep up with her.' Grace gave a wry smile. 'Rather her than me.' She noticed the expression on Alfred's face. 'I meant learning to drive the Daimler with all that traffic around, nothing to do with spending time with Matt . . . '

'How was your stroll, Grace? Did you learn everything about fossils?' Alfred's teasing tone was just what she needed. He, too spent his life upstairs as well as below stairs, so to speak. He knew how to look an awkward moment in the face.

'I'll be able to bore you rigid when we next sit down to a meal together,' she told him.

'Will we see the young gentleman again before we leave?' Alfred moved to fill the kettle. Emma's fingers were flying again, her head bent over her satin stitching.

'He's taking me out to supper tomorrow evening, so it'll be a farewell meal. A short lived friendship kind of thing.' Grace nodded her head as if underlining what she knew must be right.

'All for the best, I'm sure.'

'We must find you something pretty

to wear,' said Emma, still not looking up. 'It's not like this kind of invitation's going to come your way again. Remember Miss Rowena's emergency stock of dresses? We can look them out first thing in the morning.'

Grace felt a mix of gratitude and hurt pride. Rowena frequently lent or gave items of clothing to her and with another outing in view, and a more important one this time, it would be good to go out dressed up to the nines as Emma often said. Yet, being reminded of her lowly status gave her a pang. It decided her to unwrap that silver locket she'd mentioned to Harry and show it off for once. How fortunate it was that whenever she travelled away from home, she always packed what was to her the most precious possession in the world.

* * *

Matthew was driving his lordship to Waterloo Railway Station. Lord Carmichael sat beside him talking about his golf handicap without, Matthew decided, expecting any kind of comment from his chauffeur.

'But enough of that.' His lordship peered out at the lines of cars. 'It's a good job we left plenty of time, Matthew. I don't know what we can do about all this congestion. We'll end up with London turning into one gigantic traffic jam one day, you mark my words.'

'I hope not, my lord, if you don't mind my saying.'

Lord Carmichael chuckled. 'Perhaps I'm a pessimist. Which reminds me — how is my daughter getting on with this driving fad of hers? Is it an absolute nightmare for you?'

Matt cleared his throat. 'We've done three or four short trips around the area. So far we've only frightened one old lady who, pardon me for saying, really shouldn't have been dithering. I got out of the car and made sure she was all right.' He changed gear before they turned down the street leading to the station. 'I've just remembered something else.

There was a very impertinent bus driver last time, but Miss Rowena soon shut him up!'

'I can imagine.'

'Oh, and a lad darted out in front of us her very first time out, but Miss Rowena managed to stop. Managed very well, as a matter of fact.'

'Do you think it's worth continuing with lessons? Your uncle will be back tomorrow, so we can always see what he thinks of her progress.'

'I think Mr Hicks will be in for a surprise, my lord,' said Matt. 'I hope you don't object to me speaking my mind, but your daughter has a good feel for the car. She rarely misses a gear now.'

'Good heavens. Who'd have thought it? So you think she might develop into a safe driver?'

'I do, although I'd hate to think I'd be out of a job.'

'We couldn't do without you, Matthew. We're very pleased with your progress here, though I can't really offer you a proper promotion. Your uncle would have something to say about that, I fancy.'

'He would indeed, but thank you, my lord. Uncle Alfred will be pleased to hear what you've said.'

'Come to think of it, when we set off for the coast for our family weekend, maybe you could allow Miss Rowena to take the wheel for a few miles? Only if you feel it appropriate of course.'

Matt was giving a hand signal prior to turning right and dropping off his passenger at the station entrance. He swelled with pride at the thought of chauffeuring family members all that way, but did that mean Grace would be travelling in the car too? Did he hope this would be the case or did he not? Her rejection had hurt him, but maybe he shouldn't have accused her of looking to better herself by marrying someone from a higher class than his.

He parked as close to the entrance as he could and switched off the engine before going round to open the passenger door.

'Thank you, Matthew.' Lord Carmichael stepped onto the pavement and Matt handed him his briefcase and hat.

'I'll be here at five o'clock on the dot, my lord.'

He watched his employer make his way to his platform and wondered what it must be like to hold down an important job, with people you paid to do your bidding and a house stuffed with magnificent furniture and paintings. He'd stood in as caddy for his lordship on occasion and knew the kind of gentlemen he socialised with.

For the first time Matt understood how difficult it would be for Grace to find the right husband. She was used to eating good-quality food. She always looked smart whatever she wore, and every time she opened her mouth she couldn't help sounding like a lady. Much as it pained him to admit it, if you put her in the East End where he'd been brought up, she'd be as out of place as a peach in a rabbit stew. Maybe he didn't love her as much as he thought he had. Maybe he was suffering from a case of hurt pride.

He jumped as another chauffeur sounded his horn and drove back to Seymour House in reflective mood. When he swung the big car through the gates, young Polly was bringing in a basket of washing. He noticed how her face lit up as she saw him. That had never, ever happened with Grace.

He brought the Daimler to a halt and hopped out. 'Let me take that basket,' he called.

She put it down beside her feet. 'Miss Rowena's asking for you, Matt.'

He groaned. 'Not another driving lesson?'

She laughed. Polly had a great laugh, he thought. With a voice like hers, that was only to be expected. He found himself wanting to hear her laugh again.

'Your uncle's coming back tomorrow,' she said. 'I expect you'll be pleased to see Grace back too.'

'Not especially,' he said, picking up the basket. 'We're going our separate ways, if you really want to know.'

'I'm sorry.'

Polly looked so woebegone, Matt burst out laughing. 'Do you know what I'd like best of all in the world, Miss Polly Watts?'

She shook her head. 'To live in a castle, Mr Matthew Hicks?'

'No fear! I'd like a nice girl to sing to me and make me laugh.'

He watched a very fetching blush spread over her cheeks. After only a few days of eating Mrs Potter's wholesome meals, the Cockney sparrow already seemed to be blossoming. And when he heard Polly's peal of mirth and watched her eyes sparkle, Matt wondered if he truly had found what he wanted out of life.

6

'The grey-and-cream chiffon.' Emma spoke with conviction. She picked up the frock and held it against Grace. 'Try this one next. The pink silk isn't really you, now I see it on.' She began undoing the hooks and eyes on the pink dress so Grace could slip it over her head.

Moments later Grace stood before the cheval glass in the bedroom used by Rowena, gazing at her reflection while Emma surveyed her critically.

'This one really does suit you, you know. Maybe a necklace of some sort would be the finishing touch. Would you like me to lend you my string of pearls?'

'That's very kind, Emma. But I think I'll fetch the locket my mother left me and see how it looks. It hardly ever has an outing.' Grace turned and left the room.

'I'll put the rest of these back in the

closet,' Emma called after her.

Grace flew up the back stairs and into her small bedroom. She took the velvet pouch from beneath her pillow and slid the silver chain and heart-shaped locket out, swiftly clasping the trinket around her neck. She ran lightly downstairs again and stood in Rowena's bedroom doorway.

'Oh, my goodness! I should have known, of course.'

'Should have known what?'

'Nothing. Don't mind me. It's just that the closer you get to coming of age, the more you look like I imagine . . . um, I meant to say, the more beautiful you become.'

Grace shot her a suspicious look. 'Thanks, Emma, but I wish you wouldn't keep saying things and then seeming to regret what you said. You're making me nervous again.'

'Let's have a good look at you,' said Emma briskly. 'Turn around — that's it. Oh yes, this is definitely the right dress for you.'

'It's beautiful. Far too special for me, I think. But who could resist it?'

'Nothing's too special for you, my dear, but I hope your American admirer won't get ideas about persuading you to elope with him.'

'That's about as likely to happen as Rowena deciding to take flying lessons as soon as she's mastered driving a car.'

Grace walked slowly towards the looking-glass. 'Although, knowing what she's like, perhaps I should think of a different situation . . . '

But this time Emma made no comment whatsoever.

'I'll change back into my skirt and blouse and start putting hot water bottles in the family's and the guest beds,' said Grace. 'Unless there's something else you'd like me to do?'

'We're pretty up together, I think. Though I'd better not say that to Alfred, in case he decides we should drive back to London this afternoon after all.' She watched Grace's expression. 'I'm only joking! As if I'd stop

Cinderella from going to the ball.'

Grace gave Emma a hug. 'At least we won't have to worry about Harry's car turning into a pumpkin. I shall be back by ten o'clock but don't lock me out, whatever you do.'

'You deserve to have some harmless fun. That's what I've been saying all along.'

Grace sank down onto the bed. 'I hardly know Harry, but every moment I spend with him makes me want to be with him even more. Please don't tell Alfred though. I know my place, Emma. But I'm determined to enjoy myself this evening, and after that the future must take care of itself.'

Emma stooped and gently touched the silver locket with her forefinger. 'You must take after your mother, because you suit well-cut clothing.'

Grace noted the far-away look in Emma's eyes. 'But my mother was a little bit plump, don't you think?'

Emma straightened up with a jerk.

'Oh, Amy had a sweet tooth all right.

146

And I doubt you ever saw her in a smart outfit like this chiffon frock. Now, let's get on before Alfred asks us how long it can possibly take to select one article of clothing from a rack.'

* * *

Harry arrived on the dot at six o'clock. He drove his Bugatti up the drive and parked it next to the Daimler. Alfred hurried through the front door, ready to admire the superb saloon the young American had told him about.

'What a beauty,' he said.

'Isn't she? I can't believe my uncle trusts me with it like he does. I take very good care of her, as you can imagine.'

'And I know you'll take very good care of Grace too,' said Alfred.

Harry looked him straight in the eye. 'You bet I will. I only wish there was more time for the two of us to become better acquainted.'

Alfred bowed his head. 'You're like a

breath of fresh air. I wish I could get to the bottom of certain things but my fiancée is a stubborn woman. Grace will turn 21 soon and Emma has some information to impart. I know I shouldn't say this to you, but I do believe you have a certain young lady's interests at heart and don't just want a quick flirtation with a pretty girl on your arm.'

Harry stared back at the older man.

'Have I kept you waiting? I'm so sorry. Emma insisted I mustn't go out without a quick spray of lavender water.'

Both men watched Grace walk over the paving stones towards them. Her dark hair shone with health and there was a look of radiance about her complexion, the silver locket nestling in the perfect position above the neckline of her dress. The skirt of the smoke-grey and cream chiffon frock floated around her slender legs as she walked with assurance in high-heeled cream leather shoes. She carried a pewter-grey leather clutch bag.

'You look like you've stepped straight off the cover of one of my mother's fashion magazines,' exclaimed Harry.

'How very kind. Thank you. I've brought a scarf with me.' She looked pointedly at the open-topped car.

'Should I close the roof?' Harry looked anxious.

'Please don't do that. I'm looking forward to the fresh air.'

Alfred backed away quietly as the American took Grace's hand and kissed it. He went back into the house, closing the door behind him.

She tied the white silk scarf beneath her chin as Harry started the engine and they purred through the gates and down the lane leading to the main road.

'Where are we going?' She sat back in the crimson leather bucket seat and looked across at him.

He reached out and patted her hand. 'A little place called Kingdown which boasts a fine hotel called the Lobster Pot.'

She gave a little gurgle of laughter.

149

'That sounds lovely. Have you been there before?'

'Two or three times since it was recommended to me.'

In his turn, he shot her a glance. 'And in case you're wondering, no, I haven't ever taken some other girl there.'

'It's none of my business,' she said. 'Anyway, you've only just met me.'

'And I count myself one lucky guy to have done so.'

She didn't reply.

'You know I want to see you again.'

'We leave tomorrow after breakfast.'

'I know. Alfred told me.'

'Did he indeed?'

'He's a fine fellow. That's not all he said, either.'

Suddenly Grace felt a frisson of fear. 'Is something wrong?'

'Of course not. Gee, Grace, sometimes you remind me of a frightened baby deer. You look at me with those big grey eyes and I forget everything else in the world except the desire to protect you.'

'Oh, Harry. You know that can't happen.'

'Do I?' He checked the road was clear and pulled away from the junction.

'I've made my position plain. You have your geology project to follow through and I have to go back to London. Back to my real life.'

He didn't answer for some moments. 'From what I hear, there could be changes ahead. Alfred told me he has plans. Maybe you could be part of those plans, if you wished.'

'This is the dream of owning a little hotel?'

'Yep,' said Harry.

'I wish them nothing but the best, but it's going to be difficult for them at first and I wouldn't want to intrude on their privacy. They'll be newlyweds with a business to build up.' She kept on staring straight ahead. 'You know, Harry, being in my position isn't too awful. I have a better life than many young women do. I couldn't afford clothes like I'm wearing now if I was a stenographer or shop girl. My life would be very different.'

'But you're not one, are you? And when your Miss Rowena marries and leaves the family home, your life will change again, isn't that right?'

'My word, Alfred and you have been having an interesting discussion.'

It was Harry's turn to remain silent.

'Maybe because we both of us have your best interests at heart,' he said at last.

'You hardly know me, Harry.'

'I've known you long enough to know I've fallen in love with you.'

Grace grabbed her clutch bag and scrabbled inside for a handkerchief. Harry handed her a pristine white linen square from his pocket.

She blew her nose. 'I'll launder this and make sure you have it back again.'

'No matter. The main thing is that I have *you* back again, Grace. Whether I see you in London or down here doesn't matter to me. I think you get my drift?'

'I'm looking forward to supper,' she said.

'I'm admiring the blossom,' he said. 'Would those be May flowers in the hedgerow?'

'I think so,' she said.

'We're almost at Kingdown and I intend to buy you a glass of finest champagne.'

'Goodness,' said Grace. 'Are you sure?'

'I'm certain. Because, young lady, you deserve the best and I intend doing my darnedest to make certain that's what you get for the rest of your life.'

She spent the rest of the evening in a kind of daze, afraid to believe he meant what he said and afraid to contemplate that he didn't. She drank champagne, giggling with Harry, flirting with him and listening, fascinated, as he described his upbringing in New England. His father was a doctor and his mother grew tropical flowers in her glasshouse and insisted upon doing all the cooking and most of the housework herself.

'I like the sound of your mother,' said Grace as she nibbled a tasty morsel of lobster.

'I'm darned sure she'd like you too.'

Grace shook her head. 'She probably wants you to marry a nice girl whose folks belong to the same country club and who'd be suitable as the wife of a college professor. It's a fact, Harry.'

'My mother hates the country club. She prefers a good book of an evening. Didn't I tell you she has every one of Mr Charles Dickens's novels in her bookcase?'

Grace was won over. The sparkling wine had lulled her, softened her so she stopped being so hard on herself. She asked Harry about his younger brother who was studying law at Harvard University, her fingers toying with the beautiful silver locket as she did so. Harry's family could almost inhabit a different planet, so different was their life from that of her late parents.

Suddenly Harry leaned forward. 'That locket. It has an unusual design, doesn't it? The engraving in particular stands out.'

'Yes. I believe it must be a family coat

of arms. I imagine my father bought it from a second-hand jewellery shop or pawnbroker. I love it because my mother gave it to me.'

'Why do you say it must be second-hand?'

'Because, Harry, my parents would never have been able to afford silver jewellery. And they certainly didn't possess a family coat of arms.'

'I'd forgotten the coat of arms,' he breathed.

'What do you mean?'

'I mean that my friend Alexander Maxwell's family coat of arms looks very much like the one on your locket.'

Horrified, Grace laid down her knife and fork. Her suspicions must have been accurate after all, despite the fact she'd tried to remain positive and forget them. If Harry was right, this locket must have belonged to Lady Maxwell. Grace's mother must have stolen it, but why? Her parents, servants living in, would not have known starvation. Nor would Lady Maxwell have given away such a precious trinket to a maid-servant.

What would Harry think of her if he realised the truth of her heritage? Perhaps she came of a family of thieves and scoundrels? Grace's evening had shattered as suddenly as the shell of the lobster she and Harry were dining upon with so much enjoyment. She couldn't wait for the evening to end and found it difficult to continue sitting opposite Harry, making polite conversation.

'So many coats of arms have similarities,' she said at last, breaking the silence. 'Lord Carmichael has a book in the library at Admiral's Rest. The colours represent different qualities, professions and so on. Sometimes a family is granted a coat of arms for services to the realm or for saving someone's life. Wavy lines and mythical beasts and olive branches all crop up regularly, it seems to me.'

To her relief he seemed to swallow her explanation and backed off. 'I expect you're right. You obviously know much more about it than I do.' He closed his eyes and screwed up his face. 'Let me think ... that means the Gresham family coat of arms could consist of a stethoscope, an orchid, a fossil and a tennis racquet.'

Grace joined in his laughter and he changed the subject by asking her why the heck anyone would call a pudding by the bizarre name of spotted dick, and how would that delicacy look emblazoned on a coat of arms? She concentrated on the moment for the rest of the meal but when he escorted her out of the hotel and back to the car, she felt a twinge of regret that she wouldn't see him again after that evening. It had been a magical, if informal, couple of days but, like Cinderella, she could not expect the handsome prince to seek her out and whisk her off to his castle of dreams.

'So, ma'am, do I get to know your London address or telephone number?'

'That sunset's so wonderful, don't you think? Like a blood orange sinking into the sea.'

'Did nobody ever tell you not to answer one question with another question?'

'Oh Harry, you know I can't see you in London. Lady Cressida would be horrified if you turned up on her doorstep.'

'Why? Do I have two heads or something?'

She burst out laughing. This man was so lovely, and made her feel so happy. She pulled herself together. 'Her ladyship's idea of the perfect woman is the late Queen Victoria and she's forever at loggerheads with Rowena about lack of formality. The idea of her daughter's companion being visited by an American professor would send her straight to her bottle of smelling salts!'

'You're kidding! So, it'd be better if I was a fishmonger?'

'Probably.'

'She hasn't met me yet. We'll see about all this nonsense,' he muttered.

When he pulled up outside Admiral's Rest, Harry seemed strangely cheerful for a man who'd professed love to a girl who insisted she was out of bounds. He leapt from the car and opened her door for her, shook hands very properly and kissed her on the cheek.

'I have to drive further down the coast tomorrow to visit Lyme Regis, so I shan't be able to wave goodbye to you all.'

'I understand. I hope all goes well for you, Harry. With your fossil research, I mean.'

'Thank you. I wish I had something to give you as a token of how I feel about you, but it's kind of happened all in a rush!'

'Oh Harry, please don't say another word.'

But as Alfred opened the front door, Harry whispered 'I love you' in her ear and called a cheerful 'Good Night and please give my best wishes to Emma' before hopping back behind the wheel and driving away.

Grace stood, watching his car disappear from view and treasuring the *au revoir* whispered to her in secret. Although she knew of course he was merely being polite, because they both knew their brief but heady relationship must surely now be ended. Without a doubt she'd done the right thing. But this knowledge didn't prevent her from sobbing into her lavender-scented pillow once alone in her narrow white bed.

★   ★   ★

'Rowena! You must remember there are four wheels on a car. You've just rounded that corner using only two of them.'

'I'm sorry, Matt. I got a bit carried away.'

'At this rate we'll both be carried away on stretchers.'

Rowena giggled and drove at a sensible speed down the Great Cromwell Road. 'I felt safe though. What about you?'

'Um . . . well, I hate to admit it but in general, you're not too bad a driver.'

'For a girl, you mean?'

'I'm not walking into that one, miss . . . um, Rowena.'

'Very wise, Matt. I'm not sure what Mr Hicks will say when he finds out about my driving. They're due back any time now, aren't they?'

'So Mrs Potter told us.'

'I imagine they'll be glad to get back after all that hard work. I must remember to give Grace some peace and quiet, even though I'm dying to tell her all about my driving lessons and my new beau.'

'Indeed. If I might be so bold, miss, I had a brief word with Sir Redvers when he dropped you off after your picnic that time.'

'Really? He's amazing, Matt. So different from most of his class.'

'I really couldn't say, Miss Rowena.'

'I suppose you won't feel right about leaving out the 'Miss' bit once the others are back?'

'I think my uncle would flay me alive if he heard me address you so informally, miss. Best I get back to the old way.'

She sighed. 'In spite of the fact we live in a changing world?'

'It's not changing all that fast, as long as there's people like your mother and my uncle in it. If you don't mind my saying, miss.'

'My mother can be quite starchy at times. But she likes you, Matthew. Otherwise, I don't think she'd have allowed me to come out with you on my own to take instruction.'

'You've done very well, Miss Rowena. I really mean that. You just need more practice.' He decided not to mention what his lordship had said about giving her a chance to drive part of the way to the coast.

'Thank you, Matt. You're a good teacher. Should we head for home now? I can't remember if the next road takes us towards Marble Arch or not.'

'It does. You remember what you need to do?'

'Of course.'

Matt watched her begin the safe routine he'd instructed her in. She slowed the car to a standstill at the right position on the road, giving a hand signal just as he'd taught her. But just as she engaged first gear and drove across the right-hand carriageway, she stalled the engine. Waiting to come out of the road she was aiming for was a handsome vehicle driven by a young man whom Matt recognised as Sir Redvers Fountain, Rowena's ardent admirer.

'Cripes,' said Rowena. 'That's torn it. What's the betting on Red's Barnet standing on end, seeing me bearing down on him?'

'Um,' said Matt. 'Do you think you can pull away and stop blocking the road now, miss?

'Of course.' Cool as a cucumber, she got the engine going again, much to her instructor's relief. Her open-mouthed beau, his mother seated beside him with her eyebrows invisible under the brim of her stylish hat, was still waiting

163

at the junction as Rowena drove by, blowing kisses while she steered the Rolls Royce with her free hand down the road home.

'Do you mind me saying something, Miss Rowena?'

'Not at all.'

'How much rhyming slang do you know? You've got me worrying I've been learning you bad habits.'

'It's all right, Matt. I've been checking with the new maid to make sure I'm not saying anything that would make my mother faint.' She shot him a serene smile. 'It's a pity Red's found out about my driving, because I was hoping to surprise him by announcing it in person over dinner. I can't wait for this evening to come so I can hear what Lady Fountain thinks about his having a girlfriend who rackets around London at the wheel of an automobile.'

Matt wondered too. He also found himself wondering what Polly made of Rowena's efforts to comprehend the kind of slang a lady like her wouldn't usually hear. She was all right, was Miss Rowena, even if she did frighten the daylights out of him now and then.

Rowena steered the Rolls Royce through the courtyard gates just in time to see Alfred Hicks unfolding himself from the driver's seat of the Daimler.

'That's torn it,' she said. 'This has been quite an afternoon, don't you think, Matt? Talk about lambs to the slaughter.'

★   ★   ★

Grace was amazed and strangely moved when Rowena insisted on preparing a pot of tea for her and Emma.

'I'm afraid her ladyship will be horrified if she finds out. Please let me do it, Miss Rowena,' protested Emma.

'You've been working very hard and travelling can be exhausting, too. I'm perfectly capable of making a pot of tea, Emma. Polly has shown me exactly what to do so I shan't be long.'

Emma and Grace were relaxing in the small sitting room they used when taking a break from attending to the family's needs. The two exchanged glances.

'It seems as if we've been away for a long time instead of only a few days,' said Emma.

'I know. It's also as if once change begins, other things are also affected.' Grace's expression was wistful.

'Mrs Potter can't stop talking about the change in Miss Rowena, that's for sure.'

'It's the driving that has set the tongues wagging. I can't help noticing no one has ever suggested I should learn,' said Grace.

'The very idea! You've enough to do round here.'

'Emma, while we're on our own, could I ask when you and Alfred expect to hand in your notice? I didn't like to question you while we were away because there was so much else to think about.'

'He sprang it on me all of a sudden, didn't he? After he's spoken to his lordship, we'll know a bit more. Rest assured I'll tell you as soon as I can, and don't forget that my husband-to-be says you'll always have a home with us. Should you decide to leave Seymour House, you'll have somewhere to go to.'

Grace felt tears well up. Harry's words came into her mind and caused her to blink hard. 'I know it's something you've discussed but it's reassuring to hear it again. Thank you. Thank you both. I suppose it all hangs on what happens to Rowena, but she hasn't known Sir Redvers long so I don't suppose anything can happen there until the protocol has been attended to.'

'The months ahead should be interesting. Finding a suitable property to lease will probably take up a lot of Alfred's time, though he tells me he already has his eye on a couple of places.'

'So when do you plan to be married?'

'Not until mid-summer, I fancy. It'll be a very quiet affair of course.'

'Not if Rowena and I have anything to do with it. And Mrs Potter will be sure to make you a delicious wedding cake.'

Emma smiled. 'You and I have a bond, Grace. I'll never forget your dear mother and how her friendship helped me settle in here after I was widowed. That was a difficult time for me. Whenever I forgot to do something she'd quietly put it right and never went on at me.'

Grace nodded. 'She used to say similar things to me about you, when I was old enough to understand. She told me how grateful she was when Lord and Lady Carmichael took the three of us in after we left Edinburgh.'

She held her breath, hoping to learn more yet dreading how Emma might react to this mention of Amy and John Walker's previous time in service. Perhaps she was afraid to shatter the love and pride she knew Grace retained for the parents she'd known for such a brief period.

But Rowena came through the door, bearing a tray laden with crockery and a plate of fruitcake. 'Your afternoon tea is served, ladies,' she said, her tray wobbling as she approached.

Grace leapt up to relieve her of her burden, saying, 'Is there no end to your talents?'

'I could become accustomed to this,' said Emma. 'Many thanks, Miss Rowena.'

'Where's Alfred?' Grace enquired.

Rowena butted in. 'I expect he has Matthew by the throat, scolding him for letting a scatty young woman anywhere near the controls of his beloved Rolls Royce. Just wait till I get behind the wheel of the Daimler!'

'I can't wait to hear all about your lessons,' said Grace. 'Her ladyship is out just now, I gather.'

Rowena rolled her eyes. 'She's gone to her dressmaker's. I refused to accompany her because of my driving lesson.

Anyway, it's much more fun being with you two.'

News was exchanged in different ways over the remainder of that day. Alfred Hicks gulped and wrung his hands in despair when Matthew gave him a watered-down version of Rowena's early efforts when taking to the road. Grace enjoyed Rowena's tales of the poor car lurching along the highway before she got what Matt called 'a feel for the engine'. The way Rowena described how she'd surprised her new beau, Sir Redvers, and his haughty mother also made her chuckle.

'Red has already telephoned to compliment me on extricating myself from an awkward situation. He's so sweet, Grace,' said Rowena, her eyes giving away her feelings. 'If only I was the kind of girl who longed to marry and settle down.'

'Maybe, because you're not desperate to find a husband, he finds you different from a lot of other girls and that's one of the things that so attracts him to you,' said Grace, wondering if she dared mention Harry Gresham.

'I love being with him. I don't want to lose him, but can you really see me holding luncheon parties and playing croquet with my cronies?' Rowena pulled a face.

'It's early days, Ro. If the two of you are meant to be together, that's what will happen. But you don't need to have the same kind of lifestyle as her ladyship does. You of all people should recognise that.'

'Thank you, Grace. Yes. I should be thankful for meeting such a delightful young man. Oh, wouldn't it be wonderful if you could fall in love too!'

Grace got up and pretended to straighten a picture hanging on the wall behind Rowena. She couldn't bring herself to speak for fear of bursting into tears. Her emotions mustn't be allowed to get the better of her and she felt relieved when Rowena changed the subject. It didn't help her poor bruised heart though.

'Mr Hicks and my father are closeted in the drawing room. Do you know what's going on, Grace? Did something happen at Admiral's Rest?'

7

Grace bit her lip. 'I don't think it's up to me to discuss other people's business, Ro. Please don't try to force me. I'm sure we'll hear soon enough.'

Rowena gave her a critical look. 'So you do know something — it's more change, isn't it?'

'Nothing stays the same forever.'

Rowena leaned forward. 'I understand that. You look as though you're keeping secrets, Grace. I'm spilling my news all over the place, telling everyone how wonderful my lovely Red is and how excited I am about learning to drive; but if you want to tell me anything, I promise faithfully I won't break your confidence. You're my best friend, Grace. I think the world of you. If ever I did become married, I'd want you to come and live with us.'

Grace stared at her. 'I know you

mean well, Ro. Please don't think I'm ungrateful, but your husband — whoever he might be — wouldn't necessarily want me around. I'd love to be invited to visit you of course!'

Rowena pouted. 'Come to think of it, the situation probably won't arise. Lady Fountain looked so horrified to see me behind the wheel of the Rolls Royce, she's probably told Red he'll be disowned if he dares propose marriage to such a hoyden. She's probably at this very moment trying to dissuade him from taking me out to dinner this evening and suggesting he telephone one of those simpering debs he tells me he can't stand.'

'Would you like me to fetch your diary so we can look at your engagements together before I go and unpack my case and wait for your mother? Emma reminds me Lady Cressida will want to know exactly what the three of us achieved while we were down at the coast.'

Rowena gave Grace a wicked grin.

'Does she, now? It sounds like Emma and Mr Hicks achieved something rather important. Something life-changing, wouldn't you agree, Grace?'

'Oh, I . . . um, I think there's been a kind of understanding between them for a while now. But neither appears to have wanted to say anything out loud.'

Rowena sighed. 'Sometimes I wish I could be more like that.'

'More discreet, do you mean? Then you wouldn't be you, would you? If you want my opinion, I can see a change in you even after this short time you've known Sir Redvers. You'd never have prepared a tray of tea like that before — not even just for you and me. And as for the driving, look how you rolled up your sleeves and got on with that too. Whatever Lady Fountain might think, I shall be surprised if Sir Redvers doesn't propose to you before the season's over.'

'Goodness, Grace. I wonder if you really will be proved right.'

'I'll go upstairs and fetch your diary.'

Rowena got to her feet. 'No. I'll fetch my diary. You stay there. From now on, I want you to remain as my companion and friend and not my maid. If I can learn to drive, I can learn to sew. If I can make a pot of tea, I can learn simple cooking.'

Grace sat, mouth open, hardly able to believe what she heard coming from a young lady many considered to be a spoilt madam born with a silver spoon in her mouth.

'If changes really are taking place, I want to prove I can be helpful in more ways than one. I can hardly go on insisting I support women's rights when at home I'm being waited on hand, foot and finger by other females, now can I?'

Grace decided not to say a word, not even to Emma, after Rowena's declaration. It sounded too good to be true, but time would tell, and she would certainly have a hard job convincing Lady Cressida of the wisdom of turning over such an impressive new leaf.

But Grace, having lived through the

Great War, knew how much women could achieve given the chance. The sheltered lives of upper-class families such as the Carmichael clan might well not be able to continue as they had done. Emma had told her that Seymour House possessed fewer than half the domestic and outdoor staff it had employed two decades ago. Rowena's new enthusiasm for a more relaxed regime wouldn't necessarily please her parents, especially her mother. And the daughter of the house wouldn't have the spare time to help with domestic duties as well as undertake the many social engagements looming over the next months.

Later, when Rowena had left for her dinner engagement, Grace unpacked her bits and pieces upstairs in her bedroom. Suddenly she stopped and held the velvet pouch containing her locket against her cheek. If only she could be sure of the truth. Emma knew something, Grace was certain of that. Ever since the housekeeper's closeness to Alfred Hicks had increased and slowly become public knowledge, she'd been a little careless in certain ways. Grace had the definite feeling Emma had been on the verge of saying something significant but had changed her mind at the last moment.

And Grace still couldn't believe how Harry Gresham had apparently fallen for her. His compliments, his admiring glances, and most of all his tender kisses had cocooned her in a dream world for far too brief a period. For all his protestations, she couldn't see how he could possibly want to pursue someone of her lowly status. And her stomach lurched at the thought of Harry questioning Lady Maxwell, mother of his friend, only to discover that former employees Mr and Mrs Walker had left the Edinburgh mansion under a big black cloud. He'd be sure to run a mile in the other direction rather than have anything more to do with Grace once he knew that.

Almost without realising what she did, Grace took the locket from its velvet nest and weighed the solid silver heart in the palm of one hand. She hadn't pulled the two halves apart for many years, knowing there was no lock of hair or photograph contained within. But there was something engraved on the inside and her heart thumped alarmingly in her chest as she recalled the name Harry had mentioned while reminiscing about his stay in the Edinburgh household.

The clasp sprang back. Grace held up the open locket to the light and read the initials inscribed on the smooth silver of the left half. *I A M*. Lady Iona Maxwell, very probably Iona Alexandra Maxwell, given her son was called Alexander. But that didn't make sense. Because the date inscribed on the right-hand side was 1887. If that indicated the year of Lady Iona's birth, she would have been seventeen years of age when Grace's parents left for London with their baby daughter in 1904. Iona's married name had to be Maxwell, but how had she carried the Maxwell surname from birth?

Grace frowned and shook her head. She was torturing herself, trying to convince herself Harry had got the wrong end of the stick as to a possible link between her and the Maxwell family. And the more Grace tried to disprove his wild notion, the more tangled the situation became.

How long had it been since Harry Gresham first met his friend Alexander's mother, anyway? He'd been invited to stay with the family and noticed his hostess's portrait, painted when she'd been a much younger woman, hanging on the wall. He'd admired the youth and beauty of the young Lady Maxwell. Now, seven or eight years later, again away from home, he'd met a young woman with dark hair and grey eyes and who maybe bore a passing resemblance to the debutante in the painting. He'd fallen for Grace, or so he maintained, and confused the 20-year-old Grace with the young Lady Iona of the portrait. Perhaps when he'd been an impressionable student far from home,

he even had a secret crush on her ladyship but hadn't dared confess such a
scandalous thing.

As Grace contemplated this possibility, she still couldn't come up with a
convincing explanation as to how the
silver locket bearing the initials *I A M*
had come into the possession of a
servant. Maybe she should parcel up
the locket and chain and send them
back to the family, thus salving her
conscience. Surely Alfred Hicks would
know how to seek out the postal
address. As soon as the idea came to
her, Grace felt a wave of relief. The
silver locket would be back with its
rightful owner and hopefully she could
put her whirlwind romance with an
American professor, once again lonely
and far from home, right out of her
mind. That left her free to concentrate
on curbing Rowena's unexpected rush
of selflessness towards her fellow men
(and women) as well as able to help
Emma plan her new future as Mrs
Alfred Hicks.

But the restlessness she'd been experiencing since Harry Gresham spoke to her from behind the fence and walked into her life wouldn't leave her alone. She recalled Matt's plain speaking as he forecast her bleak future once Miss Rowena left her parents to become the bride of whichever suitor gained her hand. But his assumption that Emma would step into Mrs Potter's shoes when the cook retired didn't now apply. Emma was poised to leave her position anyway. The household would be lacking two of its most loyal and hardworking members once Alfred and Emma moved on.

Grace sank down on her knees. Resting her arms on the fluffy white candlewick counterpane, she cradled her head and let the tears flow for the second time in two days.

*   *   *

Harry Gresham walked past the closed gates of Admiral's Rest on his way to the beach. He'd spent three whole days in Lyme Regis and taken a liking to the place. The fossils and shells he'd obtained were safely stored in cases inside his house and he needed to spend time writing up his notes. Now that he was back at Sea Breezes and Grace and the others had returned to London, he felt strangely bereft. Previously he'd enjoyed the novelty of taking over a seaside cottage and not being bound by his academic timetable. Now, all he could think about was Grace Walker and the strange desire he had to investigate a situation that not only intrigued him but also gnawed at him.

Clearly, Grace was uncomfortable about his theory that she might be linked in some way with his friends. She'd come clean over the fib she told him. As it happened, he couldn't care less what her name was, except that her own suited her so well, fitting her serenity and her sweet personality. She had a feisty side to her too. He liked that. A lot of the young women he met when his parents succeeded in dragging him to parties could do nothing but smile inanely and flutter their eyelashes at him. Nor was he overly enthusiastic about the flappers, who he considered often seemed too noisy and vulgar for his liking.

Harry's mother had accused him of being far too picky when it came to selecting a girlfriend. Maybe so. But having met Grace, he knew she was right for him, and he had a sneaking suspicion she cared a little bit about him too. Despite her protestations about not being good enough for him. That was just plain stupid. And Grace certainly wasn't stupid, because she knew lots of stuff he hadn't a clue about and her way of speaking would charm the birds off the trees. She was a lady through and through. Anyone could see that. His mother had better approve!

As Harry stepped onto the shingle he'd last walked upon with Grace holding his arm, he knew exactly what he had to do. He needed to visit Edinburgh and see if he could solve this mystery over Grace Walker's startling likeness to Lady Iona Maxwell. If he was totally out of order then fine — he could tell her he'd been mistaken, apologise for worrying her and beg her forgiveness. He might even be able to discover stuff about Grace's late parents that she would treasure for the rest of her life.

It was a heck of a long shot but he had a gut feeling he was going to be proved right. And although he hadn't dared put into words and reveal what his true suspicions were to Grace, he was fully aware of the dangerous ground upon which he planned to tread.

This plan depended, of course, on whether the Maxwell family were in Edinburgh and not travelling elsewhere. It would be great to see them all again, though he doubted he'd find Alexander at home. On second thought, it might be easier to navigate this potentially awkward situation without his old friend being around. He could hopefully catch up with his pal a little later in the summer, in London maybe. Alexander was a bit of a social animal, unlike Harry in many respects, but the two got on really well.

Harry looked up at the gulls hovering over the waves and felt a twinge of nostalgia for New England. That was something else to worry about where Grace was concerned. Would she — could she — accept a marriage proposal from a man who lived on a different continent? She might not possess kin of her own, but she had a heck of a lot of affection for Emma and Alfred. And weren't her guardians kind of surrogate parents in a different kind of way? She'd also told him she and Rowena had been brought up together almost like sisters. Almost.

There was plenty of snobbery in his homeland but thank goodness his folks never subscribed to all that kind of stuff. Grace could be her own sweet self if he took her over there as his wife. He laughed out loud, sending the gulls squawking with indignation as the wind carried his guffaw away. How the heck could he be thinking so far ahead, after such a short acquaintanceship with a young lady? But Harry knew he'd found something very precious.

He'd get on to the railway station first thing in the morning and see when he could take a train to Edinburgh. If he rang Glenbarrie House he might even cadge an invitation to stay over a night or two but come to think of it, maybe he'd play safe and opt for a hotel. If he happened to overplay his hand, he might be grateful for a get out clause.

Harry picked up a flat pebble and balanced it in the palm of his hand. If he skimmed it and made it bounce three times, that would mean Grace loved him. He watched the stone soar over the waves and roared with delight as it bounced. Once. Twice. Three times. *She loves me, she loves me not, she loves me!* He shouted the words out loud, turned his back on the gently surging sea and began climbing the cliff path towards his temporary home and his bread and cheese and cider supper.

★   ★   ★

Grace walked into the kitchen at Seymour House to find Mrs Potter in her usual place at the head of the table, with her shoulders slumped. She was staring at the big teapot as if it had suddenly grown a pair of wings.

'Are you all right, Mrs Potter?'

The Kitchen Queen, as the other employees liked to call her, sat up straight and focused on the newcomer. 'I've had better days, my dear.'

Grace pulled out a chair but remained standing. 'Is this something to do with Emma's news?'

Mrs Potter nodded. 'I'm pleased for her and for Alfred too, of course I am, but I never thought they'd be the ones leaving before I cook my last joint of beef at Seymour House.'

'Why don't I make us a cup of tea? I see you've got the kettle simmering.'

'You're a good girl. Yes, I'm sure a cuppa will make me feel better. But I can't bear the thought of trying to get used to new staff. Emma was here when I first started cooking for this family. Who could possibly replace her? Tell me that!'

'They say no one's indispensable, but I have to agree with you. There's going to be a big hole to fill where that pair's concerned.'

'And who are they going to take with them? I suspected something was up when I saw Mr Hicks looking at properties in the paper a while back. He'll need staff too. Maybe Matthew will go with his uncle. And what about young Polly? Anyone with half an eye can see she's head over heels about Matthew even if he can't see it. She's a quick learner too, that little girl, though don't tell her I say so.'

Grace felt a jolt, part pleasure and part surprise. Why she felt like this, she didn't really know, except that if Matthew felt the same, there seemed no reason why these two shouldn't become a couple. In her own case, she'd fallen for someone unobtainable, despite Harry's protests to the contrary. She reached for two cups and saucers, poured milk into the cups and waited for the kettle to start whistling.

'My Ernest wants me to give up working soon. Maybe it's best I give my notice in too.'

'Oh, no!' Grace couldn't believe what she was hearing. 'You can't leave us now, Mrs Potter. Please don't make a hasty decision. I'm not at all sure Matt will want to leave Seymour House anyway. You know how mad he is about motorcars and if he stays, he's sure to take over from his uncle and move into the accommodation above the old stables. Don't you think so? And if you're right about Polly and Matt, she's hardly likely to give in her notice.'

'I suppose that's true.' Mrs Potter watched Grace pour boiling water into the big brown teapot. 'Maybe I'll become used to the idea of newcomers — if it's possible to get people to work for so little money,' she said. 'Folk aren't so keen to go into service these days.'

'There'll be someone,' said Grace, hoping to raise Mrs Potter's spirits. 'Lord and Lady Carmichael are good employers, and being so close to the West End is bound to attract people.' She placed a cup of tea in front of the cook. 'Please don't desert us. You're one of the few people who've known me since I was a little girl.'

Grace placed her own cup and saucer on the table and sat down opposite the cook.

'Tell me, dear,' said Mrs Potter. 'If Alfred and Emma asked you to go with them and help build their new business, would you be tempted? I won't tell anybody what you say, but with all this chatter about Miss Rowena's new beau and whether she might marry him later on this year, I've been wondering if you're feeling this could be the right time to make a break?'

'My goodness, it's far too soon to wonder about Miss Rowena and whether she'll marry or not. I'm sure you've heard her views on the role of a wife almost as often as I have.'

Mrs Potter laughed. 'We've had the occasional conversation. But she did tell me that her wish to learn to drive was a way of impressing this young gentleman of hers.'

'That's as may be. Now, should we think about the menus for the next few days?'

'Her ladyship gave me some suggestions for this supper party at the weekend, but I'm not sure she's thought about what's in season and what isn't. Shall I read the list out loud?' Mrs Potter reached for her big red notebook, its cover marked with greasy thumbprints and dulled by years of proximity to countless siftings of flour and hundreds of eggs being whisked to a froth. She riffled through the pages until she reached her latest entry.

* * *

Harry Gresham was enjoying the convertible motorcar he was lucky enough to be using during his stay in England. It still seemed strange to be driving on the opposite side of the road from back home though. Once he reached the London suburbs, a feeling of excitement built inside of him as he wondered what kind of reception he'd receive when he knocked upon the door of Seymour House.

He'd rung his uncle to tell him how grateful he was for the use of the car and had casually dropped into conversation the fact that Lord and Lady Carmichael were his neighbours down in Dorset.

'I haven't had the pleasure of becoming acquainted yet,' he'd said. 'But, as I have to be in London to visit the British Museum, I wondered if you could let me know their address so I can call and hope to find her ladyship at home.'

Harry muttered the address under his breath as he concentrated upon threading his way across an area of London he'd never driven through before. But Marble Arch proved an excellent landmark and soon he was turning into a quiet residential street and slowing down to park under a leafy tree halfway along the right road.

He hopped out and marched purposefully down the pavement until he reached the imposing main entrance of Seymour House, its name engraved on the exterior stonework.

'This is one swell townhouse,' he muttered to himself, hastening up the stone steps leading to the front door.

He rang the bell and waited, on the verge of ringing a second time when he heard footsteps, and the heavy door opened to reveal a tall man who Harry instantly recognised as Alfred Hicks.

'Mr Hicks, it's good to see you again so soon.'

Alfred nodded. 'Mr Gresham, sir. How may I help you?'

Harry felt puzzled. Was this the man with whom he'd chatted about motor-cars so recently? He seemed so stiff and starchy in his dark suit, his hair slicked down. What a contrast.

Harry smiled at the butler and offered his calling card. 'You might be aware I already left my card at Admiral's Rest, but I happened to be in town and wondered if it was possible to speak to Grace.'

Mr Hicks took the card. 'Please step inside, Sir. You might like to wait in the small drawing room while I see if her ladyship is available.'

Her ladyship? Harry removed his hat and followed the butler, feeling as if he'd fallen into a British movie without knowing the script. He supposed etiquette demanded Lady Carmichael should be informed of his calling but if she was busy, did that mean he couldn't see Grace? He stood, hands in pockets, staring at a portrait of a woman who could have been anyone for all Harry knew. The lady reminded him of the photographs he'd seen of Queen Victoria and to him she seemed equally forbidding. No doubt she was an ancestor. Wasn't all the British nobility related to royalty if you trawled back far enough?

Alfred Hicks walked back into the room. 'Her ladyship thanks you very much for calling, Sir, but regrets she's about to leave for an important appointment.'

'So, could I call back later? I have to visit the museum and that's not far from here. How about Grace? Might I see her, Mr Hicks?'

'I'm sorry, Mr Gresham, but that's impossible. I'm sure Lady Carmichael will be pleased to receive you if you happen to be staying at the coast while the family is in residence at Admiral's Rest.'

The cold shoulder! Harry surely recognised that when he saw it. This clever idea of his wasn't turning out the way he'd imagined when planning it. He'd heard of British reserve, but hadn't imagined London society behaviour would be so different from the relaxed manners of the household members he'd met in Dorset.

'Is that impossible period, or impossible just at the moment?'

Alfred Hicks hesitated.

'I mean, is it impossible full stop? Come on, you understand what I'm asking, Mr Hicks.'

'The family and staff are all very busy preparing for a party at the weekend, Sir.'

'Two minutes with Grace, Mr Hicks! That's all I'm asking.'

Alfred looked uncomfortable. 'Best not to press the matter, I think, Sir.'

Harry heaved a sigh. 'All right. I get the picture. I'm sorry if I've made you embarrassed in any way.' He pulled on his hat and stood waiting to be shown through the door.

Mr Hicks whispered something after he bade Harry farewell. It sounded like 'I'm sorry but it's for the best,' though Harry couldn't be sure and wasn't about to question the man who was, after all, only doing his job.

The young American walked slowly

across the road, his dejection blotting out the sunshine from the day to which he'd looked forward with such enthusiasm during his car journey. He was wondering whether to move his vehicle or to leave it where it was and walk to the museum when he heard someone call his name.

Whirling around, he saw a young woman, a delightful blonde with one of those flapper haircuts and wearing an emerald-green dress with an unusual blue-ribbon trim. She was a beauty all right, and crossing the road towards him, but why was she waving and hollering after a stranger?

'Mr Gresham? You don't know me but I'm Rowena Carmichael.' She held out her hand.

Bemused, he took it, remembering his manners. 'The Honourable Rowena?'

'Never mind the formalities,' she said. 'I'm so sorry about that misunderstanding back there. I'm afraid my mother, her ladyship, lives life in little compartments. She has her London face on and consequently didn't take the trouble to question why you'd taken the trouble to call upon us.'

'It's OK. Your butler told me how busy you all are. But how did you know I'd arrived?'

Rowena drew his attention to a small garden area. 'Let's sit down across there. It'll be more private.'

Even more bemused, Harry followed her to a bench hidden from onlookers by sheltering foliage.

She turned to face him. 'The calling card you left at Admiral's Rest was amongst a pile brought back by Mr Hicks. I took a look through them and yours was the only name I didn't know. So when I heard Mr Hicks speaking to you when I was about to come downstairs, I recognised your name and hung around to find out what happened.'

'Tell me, Rowena, has Grace mentioned me at all?'

'No. But I got the feeling something happened while she was away. We know each other's moods after all these years being brought up together. She's such a very loyal, very discreet person, Mr Gresham. I adore her and I know she probably wouldn't want to push her own feelings to the forefront. I imagine you're here because of her and not merely to pay a duty call upon my mother?'

'You bet your life! I've fallen in love with Grace.'

Rowena flung her arms around him. 'That's wonderful news, though I'm going to kill her for not telling me first!'

'Whoa!' Harry chuckled. 'It's not as simple as that. Grace has this darned stupid idea that she's not good enough for me. Can you imagine that? When you've just told me how much she means to you and your family?'

Rowena wrinkled her nose. 'I hate to say this but, yes, I can imagine why she'd consider herself unable to enter into a relationship with you. It's all about status.' She raised her hand to stop him protesting. 'I'm not for one minute saying she's right. Grace is a lady through and through but because her parents were servants, she feels that's very much her place in life too.'

'I know she's much, much more than a servant to you all. But how do I convince her I don't care two hoots about her background?'

'First of all, you need time alone with her. Are you free this afternoon?'

'I have no appointments.' Harry watched Rowena's face.

'Then be at the entrance to the Wallace Collection at two o'clock. That's Hertford House, just minutes away from here.' She pointed in its direction. 'I shall convince Grace of my need to take some fresh air and I'll deliver her to you and wander off so you can talk. But you mustn't take longer than half an hour. I'm due to go out visiting with my mother at three o'clock and it's more than my life is worth to be late.'

8

'It's not like you to suggest a walk so close to an outing with your mother, Rowena.'

'I have my reasons. Trust me, Grace.'

Grace felt a pang as she remembered Harry using those same words to her and how she'd know her heart would be safe with him were it not for the fact of her humble birth. She would have gone to America with him — she'd have gone to the ends of the earth with him, but how would his parents view his marriage to a young woman of low status and with hardly a penny to her name?

She frowned as Rowena took her arm and hurried her along the pavement towards the Wallace Collection. 'Are we going inside? They have some beautiful exhibits here but I thought you disliked looking round museums. Is this your new beau's influence?'

But Rowena didn't answer. She came to a standstill outside the building and someone was calling Grace by name. She turned around and there he was, and all the love in her heart filled her with warmth and delight as she felt Harry's arms envelop her.

'My beautiful Grace. I can't be without you. Tell me you feel the same.'

Grace gasped and looked around for Rowena.

'She's melted away,' said Harry. 'If it weren't for Miss Rowena, I wouldn't be standing here now with the girl I want to make my wife.'

Grace stiffened. 'Oh, Harry, you know that's impossible.'

She saw the stricken look on his face.

'So, does that mean you don't love me like I love you?'

'I do love you, Harry. That's why I can't possibly become your wife.'

He linked her arm in his and led her gently away from the building and towards the gardens in the middle of the square.

'Did you see Lady Cressida?'

'No. She didn't deign to grace me with her presence. Luckily, your friend heard Mr Hicks speaking as he booted me out and she came after me when I left with a flea in my ear.'

'I'm so sorry, Harry, but I'm afraid that's how things must be. I'm a servant. You're a college professor. Lady Cressida has strict boundaries regarding class.'

'Her ladyship had no idea why I was here. I didn't take kindly to her treatment of me but to be fair, I did call out of the blue. To my surprise, it was Alfred Hicks who refused to let me see you.'

'I see. He's a walking encyclopaedia of etiquette and he did the right thing of course.'

'Do I detect a tinge of regret in your words?'

Grace turned her head to gaze in the opposite direction. 'It's true he wasn't so formal down at the coast but, he has my best interests in mind. You have no idea what it would be like for you, being married to someone like me.'

'Oh, believe me, I think it'd be pretty darned good. And my folks would adore you. I've already told you that. Come with me, Grace! I want us to be together. Tell her ladyship you're moving to New England and need to hand in your notice.'

Grace stood and he jumped to his feet and took her hands in his. 'You'll say yes?'

She watched his eager face, his eyes shining with love and hope. It was with a very heavy heart that Grace Walker shook her head and walked away from Harry Gresham, back to the life where she knew she belonged, even if it was a situation she might not wish to continue.

He didn't chase after her. But he called something and though a sudden gust of wind lifted his words and whisked them away, Grace heard Harry's determined vow to make her change her mind.

She met Rowena on the pavement outside Seymour House.

'Where is that adorable young man?' Rowena asked. 'Did you come to an understanding? I do hope so.'

'I shan't be seeing him again.' Grace heard the desolation in her voice and willed herself not to break down.

'But you must. I can tell what you mean to one another, despite such a brief acquaintanceship, because I know how Red and I feel about each other. You're the one who'd make a wonderful wife, Grace. It's you who should be marrying Harry Gresham while I rattle around London with Red. I don't want to lose you but I realise how trapped you are by circumstances.'

Grace blinked hard. She hadn't previously thought of herself in that way but hearing the words out loud brought her position into the harsh glare of daylight.

Yet when she helped Rowena change her dress ready to accompany her mother to afternoon tea with a relation in Hampstead, she knew there was no escape. And when she told Emma how the American had turned up out of the blue and how she'd dealt with his marriage proposal, she wasn't surprised to hear Emma assure her she'd done the right thing. If it truly was the right thing, then why, wondered Grace, did she feel as though her heart had turned into a wooden block?

★   ★   ★

Harry was in no mood for browsing fossil collections, much as he loved the things. He needed to walk, so walk he did. He walked the length of Park Avenue towards the Serpentine and found a Lyons Corner House where he nursed a cup of black coffee, ignoring tasty sandwiches and cakes. But it wasn't in Harry's nature to give up on something so dear to his heart. This was why he'd refused to study medicine and make his parents proud. He'd opted for geology and the quiet life of an academic, leaving high grades and tennis championships to his younger brother.

His coffee cooled as an amazing idea came to him. He threw some coins on the table, picked up his hat and jammed it on his head, going out into the busy street and turning in the direction he'd come.

With the help of a friendly London policeman he met en route, he arrived back at his car and drove to his uncle's house, losing his way only once and having to stop and ask a hotel doorman for directions. He felt a sense of relief as he pulled up outside yet another spacious townhouse on a quiet, leafy street. His knock on the door was answered without delay.

An elderly woman who looked to him as if she'd been alive for at least a century showed Harry into the study, where his uncle sat at a writing desk.

'My word, young Harry. My housekeeper and I didn't expect you for dinner until seven, but you're welcome nonetheless.'

Harry shook hands with Edward Rossiter and didn't waste any time.

'Uncle Eddie, could you advise me of the best way to travel to Edinburgh, Scotland? I guess that's a long way for me to drive your beautiful car.'

'It's also a long way to travel to inspect yet more fossilised insects.'

Harry grinned. 'I've met a girl.'

'I thought as much. So you're chasing after her and visiting her home?'

'Not in so many words . . . '

'I think,' said Uncle Eddie, 'you and I had better take a wee dram while you satisfy an old man's curiosity as to why your face lights up like a Christmas tree when you tell me you've met a girl. In her last letter to me, your dear mother was bemoaning the fact that you seemed on course to remain a bachelor, lurking among your collection of dusty fossils, as she put it, for the rest of your life.'

★　★　★

Harry armed himself with several news-papers and magazines before taking his seat upon the London and North Eastern Railway service from London to Edinburgh.

His uncle had acquainted him with some of the landmarks to look out for during his journey, and of course Harry spent much of the 392 miles between the two capital cities daydreaming about his possible future with Grace. If his suspicions were true, she'd be shocked; but once she recovered from that shock he hoped to receive a different answer from her when he next popped the ques-tion. He chatted for a while to an elderly couple travelling as far as York to visit their married daughter, and enjoyed a dry sherry and a good lunch of Brown Windsor soup and Dover sole in the restaurant car while gazing out at yet more scenery as he ate.

He alighted eight and a half hours after boarding, overnight bag in hand, and still unsure whether to take a cab and check into his hotel or to head straight for the Maxwell residence. Thanks to Uncle Eddie's practical character, Harry had made a telephone call to the household the evening before, saying he was visiting Edinburgh and would like to renew his acquaintance with the family. His friend's parents were attending the theatre, but the person answering the telephone assured him Lady Maxwell had no engagements for the next couple of days and that his message would be relayed to her. Harry's uncle had recommended a central hotel to him and telephoned to reserve one single room for two nights.

At least, thought Harry, he wouldn't be barrelling in to the Maxwell residence unannounced. And at once he knew he couldn't wait any longer. This was an extremely daring thing which he was about to do and, travel-stained though he might be, but he needed to speak to Lady Iona and if necessary ask if he might take her to luncheon the next day, should it prove difficult to speak of such a delicate matter in her home.

He went straight to the cab rank and gave the driver the address. The cabbie provided a running commentary on the city as he drove his American passenger, but Harry missed some of the comments, his ear not tuned into the man's way of speaking. He did manage to grasp that the large statue he passed was that of Prince Albert on horseback, and that Queen Victoria herself had unveiled the imposing memorial.

When Harry paid off the driver and stood looking up at yet another magnificent property, he wondered whether the mystery nagging at him was on the verge of being explained. But he needed to tread carefully; and even as he rang the doorbell and winced at the loudness of the chime, he wondered if he'd totally lost his sanity and should make no mention of the matter but merely write off his visit as a courtesy call. His dad would use the expression 'hornets' nest' and as this thought entered his mind, he hid a grin and composed his features into a polite smile as the door opened.

A butler took his hat and suitcase and, at Harry's whispered request, showed him to a small cloakroom where he could wash his hands and comb his hair before meeting his hostess.

Lady Iona received him in a pretty sitting room on the first floor, rising to greet him, hands outstretched. He reckoned the view was to die for — and that included her ladyship as well as the Edinburgh landscape.

'Harry Gresham, after such a long time! I'm afraid my husband is dining at his club, and you won't be surprised to hear Alexander isn't at home.' She offered her cheek for Harry to kiss.

'I didn't expect he would be, your ladyship. Last time I heard from Alex he was about to join his regiment in Yorkshire.'

'I suppose it was inevitable for our son to follow the family tradition and join the military. But Harry, do please call me Iona. There's no need to stand on ceremony.' She gestured for him to sit on the chintz-covered couch opposite her blue velvet armchair.

'Thank you. It's so good to see you again. I seem to recall being just a hare-brained student last time I visited.'

'Did you enjoy the rest of your time at Oxford?'

'Very much. I made several good friends apart from Alex.'

'You're still a bachelor?'

'Indeed I am. I believe I'm a great disappointment to my mother.' Harry wasn't ready to mention Grace yet.

'You have time to settle down, as has my son, of course. Are you still lecturing at the university?'

'I am. I enjoy living in Vermont, and it's not too distant from where my folks live now. They decided to purchase a smaller property, but it's still a lovely house. Mom's such a keen gardener and that keeps her busy.'

He watched his hostess glance at a small gold carriage clock upon the mantelpiece.

'I hope I'm not interrupting your evening too much, Iona.'

Her smile tore at his heart, reminding him so much of Grace. But he must not frighten away this lovely woman. He needed to use all his powers of tact and diplomacy.

'Not in the least! I'm delighted to have your company, Harry. I was wondering if you'd care to join me in a glass of sherry. When my husband dines at his club I normally have something on a tray. Would that suit?'

'It would be more than welcome, as long as you're sure I'm not imposing upon you.'

She rose. 'Excuse me. I'll be back in a moment.'

He rose and watched her leave the room — except he reckoned the right word was glide — before he approached the portrait he remembered from his visit more than eight years earlier. There was that sweet smile and those eyes looking at him, reminding him so much of the young woman he'd fallen in love with in Dorset. The way Grace had given him a false name — the fact that she'd chosen Maxwell — surely couldn't be pure coincidence. There must be a way he could discover what this link between her and Lady Iona was, without offending his hostess. If only he had that silver locket with him, he could place it in Iona's hand and watch her reaction. At least he could describe the jewellery in great detail, a skill gained from years of peering at ancient remains, thereby honing his powers of observance.

He was still gazing at the portrait when Iona came back into the room. 'Since you were here last, we've given up ringing when we need something. The war changed many things, but these days we still retain a small staff. My excuse is we entertain often and I'm not the best of cooks.'

'No need to make excuses — you're keeping folk in employment and that must be a good thing.'

She smiled at him again. 'Come and

sit down, Harry. The girl in that portrait has changed a lot too. She was barely seventeen at the time.'

'I'm fascinated by her, to tell the truth.' He took his seat again.

'Fascinated by how much she has changed?' Her eyes glinted mischievously and his heart flip-flopped once more.

'Now, you know that's not true! What I meant was, I met a young lady recently whose likeness to you intrigues me.'

She stared at him for moments. 'Goodness, Harry, there must be countless young women with dark hair and grey eyes.'

'Of course. But apart from colouring, this particular young woman has the same shaped face as you. Would you describe your face as heart-shaped?'

'I suppose that's true. Maybe she's a distant relation. We'll never know, I suppose.'

Harry hesitated as he heard a discreet tap on the door and a maid entered, bearing a decanter and two crystal glasses upon a silver tray. His hostess thanked the girl and asked Harry if he'd like to help them both to a glassful. They sipped their sherry and sat in silence for a while.

'Do you by any chance still have that beautiful locket you were wearing when your portrait was painted?' He held his breath.

'As it happens, I don't.' She put down her glass. 'Tell me more about Vermont. I don't for one moment believe there are no eligible young ladies in your social circle.'

Harry didn't press Iona further regarding the silver jewellery he was convinced he'd seen around Grace's neck. Somehow he had to catch her off guard. Maybe the defence she'd have been forced to erect two decades ago, if he was right in assuming she was indeed Grace's true mother, would prove easier to dismantle if he could speak to her away from her home.

He kept the conversation light-hearted. Iona asked him to top up their glasses when a cold roast beef and salad supper was served. He managed to bring the conversation back to the fact that his parents had moved from Connecticut a few years previously and asked her where her family home had been when she left to become Lord Maxwell's bride.

Her eyes widened. 'Oh, but this has always been my home,' she said. 'My husband is also my first cousin, so I abandoned being Miss Maxwell to become Mrs Maxwell.'

'You're teasing me! Originally, you must have been the Honourable Iona Maxwell and — now let me figure this out . . . Alex's dad inherited the title because there was no son to succeed, and he was the first cousin. So after you married, your husband moved in here with you. Am I right?'

'Spot on. My parents were still alive then. These days it's just the two of us. Do help yourself to more beef and potatoes, Harry. What are your plans for the rest of your stay?'

At least he knew why the unmarried Iona already bore the surname of Maxwell, thus explaining why there was no name change upon marriage. He should have thought of that possibility, but no matter. He was maybe one step further forward towards the unravelling of Grace's heritage.

'I'm staying two nights. I intend doing some sightseeing before I return to Dorset and my fossil hunting. I wonder if I might take you and your husband to luncheon tomorrow?' He held his breath, knowing if that happened, he risked being unable to steer the conversation as he wished. But he dared not make a social gaffe by inviting a married lady to luncheon without including her husband too.

'Are you inviting us because you think we're also fossils?' Her eyes were dancing again.

'Ha! Because I'd like your advice on something, and I want to say thank you for your hospitality when I came here with Alex from Oxford.'

'That's not necessary, Harry, but as my husband is playing golf tomorrow, I shall be pleased to take up your kind invitation.

★ ★ ★

Grace kept herself as busy as possible, thankful that the approach of the hectic London season meant there were hair appointments to fit in, clothes to be laundered and new outfits for her ladyship and Rowena to be tried on, approved and carefully pressed by Grace after the dressmaker delivered them. She spent her time at the ironing board, running errands, solving problems and listening to Rowena prattling either about Sir Redvers or her driving lessons.

Emma was distracted and Grace knew her thoughts often dwelled upon her forthcoming new life, although it appeared she and Alfred weren't rushing to find a property until things settled down a bit and the new maid could cope with more responsibilities. She didn't make any mention of Harry Gresham, and while Grace realised this must be for the best, she longed to talk about him. Her feelings remained strong for the young American and she feared being sent to Admiral's Rest again, knowing he was staying in the neighbouring cottage — or worse still, turning up as a dinner guest. There might as well be a wall of stone between the two of them in that particular situation. Midnight meetings in the garden would mean playing with fire, even though Grace knew Rowena would be eager to help achieve such assignations.

Rowena didn't display the same discretion as Emma did. One day while they walked to Oxford Street together, she startled Grace by asking, 'Are you quite certain you did the right thing in sending Harry Gresham away?'

Grace recovered herself enough to stammer a response. 'It's for the best. That's what Mr Hicks said to Harry, and to me, and I know he's right.'

'What nonsense. It's a pity Alfred Hicks doesn't know as much about the human heart as he does about the combustion engine!'

'That's hardly fair, is it? He proposed to Emma.'

'And look how long it took him. He's almost as old as my parents. He knows nothing about modern life.'

Grace didn't have the heart to argue. She knew full well how, because of her lowly status, in the wildly unlikely circumstances that she were to accept Harry's proposal, his parents were bound to feel stunned, angry and distant. His father might even disinherit him and leave the whole of his estate to Harry's younger brother. She couldn't bear the thought of having that upon her conscience. Nor could she bear the thought of the whispered comments behind hands and beyond earshot, along the lines of how that nice Harry Gresham had thrown away his prospects and all for the sake of a flibbertigibbet English girl he'd taken a fancy to while far from home.

With her emotions all over the place and the hectic days both at the coast and back in London, Grace had temporarily forgotten a milestone most young women would be anticipating with excitement. She would turn 21 at the weekend. But that was the day Lady Cressida was hosting a party for her closest friends and Grace would be kept busy making sure both her ladyship and Rowena sparkled like superior diamonds set amongst a coronet of glittering but less rare gems.

The weekend after that was scheduled for the first family holiday that year down at the coast. Grace had no idea whether she would be required to travel with Rowena. Fortunately both she and Matthew were busy enough not to have time to fret about the other and revisit his idea about their futures. Grace sensed he'd put the matter behind him. And the occasional remark let slip by Mrs Potter, in between complaining about the amount of work she had to do, made Grace wonder if Matt had indeed taken a shine to young Polly Watts.

But the evening before the party, while Grace sat like Cinderella shortening the straps on one of Rowena's chemises, Emma came into the workroom with a strange expression on her face.

'Are you all right? You look a bit flummoxed.' Grace knotted the thread and snapped off the end, shaking the ivory silk garment so it settled ready for her to fold.

'I don't mean to be. Have you finished with sewing?'

'Yes, thank goodness. Barring accidents, everything's in order, and Rowena's gone out to a cocktail party with Lord Redvers so I'm done for the night.'

Emma held out a cream-coloured envelope. 'We'll all be busy again tomorrow so I thought it best to bring this to you now, Grace.'

'Is it a greeting card? Oh thank you, Emma, but do you really think I should open it before the actual day? Won't that mean bad luck?'

'There'll be more than one birthday card at the breakfast table, including mine and Alfred's. This is something different. It's not from me and I'm handing it to you now because you deserve time to think about its contents.'

Grace shook the envelope. 'This is most mysterious. Do you know what's in it? It doesn't feel very heavy.'

'All I know is that it's a letter given to me by your mother for safekeeping until your twenty-first birthday.'

'My mother? Why did she not give it to me herself before she — '

'My dear, it contains information your mother decided should be kept from you until you reached maturity. I don't imagine she'd be angry with me for handing it to you so close to your twenty-first birthday.'

Grace reached for a pair of scissors and deftly sliced the envelope open. She took out a sheet of heavy white notepaper, unfolded it and began reading while Emma sank down on a wooden stool and stared at her feet, hands folded in her lap.

Grace had to read the first paragraph three times before she looked up at Emma.

'Did you know this? About the circumstances surrounding my birth?'

'Of course.'

Her face tightened. 'And you never thought to tell me?'

'Grace, please believe me when I say your mother swore me to secrecy. She asked me to fetch the letter from her bedroom drawer when she first took ill. Maybe she had a premonition about what was about to happen to her. Of course I agreed to keep the secret. How could I not? She'd confided in me that you weren't her own daughter, though it was obvious she and your father loved you as though you were.'

Grace nodded. 'I can hardly take it in. You did right to tell me now, Emma. But am I not allowed to know the identity of my real mother — the woman who gave me life?'

Emma looked away.

'Do you know?'

'I . . . I only know this person was of noble birth and aged only seventeen when she left Edinburgh to live quietly in the country and wait for you to be born. She must have confided in your mother because Amy kept in touch with her and visited her on her rare days off. It was your parents who asked if they could be the ones to bring you up. You must believe the woman who was your natural mother was anxious you should go to a good home, and she knew Amy and John would love and care for you, even if they weren't rich.'

'Because my real mother knew the scandal my arrival would have caused? I expect my maternal grandmother — or should I say her ladyship — didn't even tell my grandfather.' Grace couldn't believe how calm her voice sounded considering her mind was in such turmoil.

'I know nothing other than that everyone understood the young lady in question was going to Switzerland to attend a finishing school. Apparently, because this was a common thing to happen with girls of her class, no one asked any questions. While your mother awaited your arrival, she spent her time hidden away in a house where an aunt resided. She took pains to practise the piano, improve her knowledge of French and compose a sketchbook to show off on return.'

'Very clever. I imagine she hardly had the need to learn etiquette, coming from a background like hers. She'd have been able to sweep the whole matter under the table and get back to her life of luxury.'

Emma blinked hard. 'I know this is difficult for you to accept, my dear. But such things happen and those you think of as your parents were overcome with joy that you arrived in their lives. You should know that Amy and John thought parenthood was not to be for them until you arrived in their lives.'

Grace nodded. 'I wish they were still around, for many reasons. But now I know the truth, I have so many questions to ask.'

'I promise you I've told you as much as I know.'

'Is it possible that I'm a Maxwell by birth? We both know that my mother and father worked for a family of that name. How odd that it came so readily to my lips when Harry Gresham asked me what I was called. It's even more odd that he should be acquainted with a family of that name.'

Grace watched Emma's face, and saw the flutter of her eyelashes and the instant rush of colour to her creamy cheeks.

'You don't have to answer,' said Grace. 'I think I can draw my own conclusions. Neither you nor Amy seem to have realised that the initials I.A.M. are engraved on the back of the silver locket you handed over after Mum died. But I need to read the rest of this letter. There are instructions to follow regarding my contacting a solicitor here in London.'

'Should I leave you alone?'

'No. Stay with me, Emma. Please stay with me. I feel as though I'm in a dream at the moment and I might need you to pinch me and convince me all this is real.'

9

Harry arrived at the Maxwell residence in a cab and asked the driver to wait while he knocked at the door, his heartbeat maybe a little faster than normal, but ready to escort her ladyship to luncheon at one of Edinburgh's finest hotels. Iona came out of the house almost immediately and, his heart thumping faster, he thought again how Grace resembled this elegant woman in several ways. Iona wore a silver-grey dress and a tiny hat composed mainly of purple feathers. Her own hair was still raven's-wing dark and cut in a similar style to Grace's. Harry could barely contain his impatience, so eager was he to tell his old friend's mother all about the wonderful girl he'd met and divulge sufficient information about Grace to, he hoped and prayed, cause a reaction that would lead to the result he yearned for.

As soon as they were seated at a window table overlooking the mound topped by Edinburgh Castle, and sipping champagne cocktails, Harry patted the snow-white tablecloth and confessed his need for some advice.

'So, all along, you had an ulterior motive in inviting me to luncheon?' Iona's eyes mocked him above the frosted rim of her long-stemmed cocktail glass.

'Partly,' admitted Harry. 'It's a fact how truly grateful I was for your family's kindness to me when I was still adjusting to life at Oxford. Your son insisted I come to Scotland with him instead of staying in college, staring at the walls of my room during reading week.'

'We probably weren't strict enough about you two boys actually doing what the week was designed for, but neither of you has done too badly since,' said Iona. 'Do you know, I still have the very delightful letter your mother wrote me when she heard you'd spent a holiday with us.'

'Really? Well, maybe I'm missing that mother of mine and maybe that's why I hoped to get you on your own today and cry upon your shoulder.'

'Now I am intrigued. You don't look the crying kind to me.' Iona popped a luscious green olive into her mouth.

Harry took a deep breath. 'The truth is, I've fallen in love with someone.'

Iona laughed. 'I thought you said your mother must be despairing of you, having reached the grand old age of twenty-six and still not keeping company with any special young lady.'

'Mom knows nothing about Grace. Yet.'

Did he detect a spasm crossing Iona's face? Harry watched, almost afraid to breathe, as she took a sip of her drink and replaced the glass with a little too much care upon the snowy tablecloth.

'Grace is a very pretty name,' she said. 'It's the name I chose ... the name I'd have chosen had I produced a daughter instead of a son.'

'Really? Well, this particular Grace is more than pretty.' He leaned in closer, twirling the stem of his cocktail glass between his fingers. 'This Grace is very beautiful and I want her to be my wife — if I can persuade her to have me, that is.'

'So how did you meet this young woman? Was it at a party?'

'I happened to be outside in the garden of the cottage I'm renting in Dorset. She was out in the garden of the house next door, which is owned by her employers. It's their summer residence. I heard her voice and knowing she must be one of my neighbours, I confess to having accosted her from behind the fence.'

'So you weren't exactly behaving as a gentleman should behave? You hadn't been properly introduced to this young lady?'

'Well, I am an American, after all!'

'As if I could forget.' Iona smiled that smile he knew so well.

'We agreed to walk round to the gate

and introduce ourselves. I have to confess to being smitten with Miss Grace Maxwell.' He spoke the name that Grace originally gave him, so distinctly that he knew Iona would be quite certain it was the same name as her own.

'Are you ready to order, sir?' The waiter hovered discreetly behind Harry's important luncheon guest.

To her credit, Iona didn't hesitate in giving her choice.

'I'll have the same,' said Harry.

The waiter backed off and Harry focused his attention upon Iona. Her face remained impassive but the fingers of one hand trembled as she touched them to her lips. He ached for her. Wanted to put his arms around her and tell her he understood the anguish she must be going through, but he daren't. Not yet. Any confession needed to be made by her and he intended to try his darnedest to convince her how much Grace meant to him.

'I think . . . I hope Grace loves me too.'

'I sense a 'but' coming here.' Iona retained her composure — an ability, Harry imagined, she'd inherited not only via her genes but from spending two decades keeping a very poignant and personal secret.

'If I may, I'd like to tell you something of her background.'

He noticed an almost imperceptible tremble as Iona unfolded her linen serviette but, hating himself for causing her pain or embarrassment, he knew he must speak with openness.

'It seems her late parents were in service to an Edinburgh family, but they left this family when Grace was just a babe in arms and obtained employment with Lord and Lady Carmichael, who live in Manchester Square, London.' He watched Iona's stricken expression and almost lost his nerve, but not quite.

'The thing is, Grace feels she's not good enough for me. She's worried my parents won't accept her. She's under the impression that she's not suitable to become the wife of a man who admits to being a slightly nutty professor who's wild about fossils and shells and nature in general. Now, don't you think that's too crazy for words?'

Bowls appeared before them. Two waiters wearing immaculate white gloves served asparagus soup from a silver tureen. Harry possessed himself in patience while fresh parsley was scattered over a comma-shaped swirl of cream decorating the surface of the smooth green soup. The waiters melted away, leaving him alone with Iona. He prayed she would not get up and walk away from the table.

'This smells delicious,' he said, breaking his bread roll in two. 'The other thing is, when I took Grace out to supper in Dorset, she wore a beautiful silver pendant. Please forgive me, but I have to tell you I have a hunch it might be the one you're wearing in that portrait you have hanging in your sitting room. As soon as I saw that heavy silver chain around Grace's neck, I remembered it from the time Alex brought me to stay with you and I admired your portrait.'

Iona met his gaze, her face impassive. It was, thought Harry, one of those moments when everything seems to stop and the future hangs in the balance.

He started breathing again as she picked up her spoon. 'You Americans have an expression, do you not — something about spilling the beans? Is that what you expect from me, Harry?'

'Please, Iona, rest assured I haven't come to Scotland to shatter your marriage. Nor do I have any intention of saying a word to Alex or to anyone in the world apart from Grace, if you'll only permit it. I guess you did what you had to do and not what you really wanted to do. I know you must have had your daughter's best interests at heart. I can only imagine how tough the whole business must have been for you.'

Iona inclined her head. 'Have you visited Grace at Seymour House?'

He noticed the telltale brightness in

her eyes as she spoke but his heart bumped faster as he realised his suspicions had indeed been accurate.

'I tried to but I came away with my tail between my legs because I asked to see someone who's perceived as a servant.' He made a wry face. 'I have no illusions. I didn't expect Lady Cressida to drop everything and receive some unknown American who happened to be renting the cottage next door to her second residence. She had no idea what my reason was for calling at her London address. But after I asked to see Grace and was refused, the butler, who I'd met in Dorset, whispered to me that it was all for the best. Doesn't that tell you something?'

Iona nodded. Bit her lip.

'My family are not out of the top drawer. They're ordinary folk who've had to work hard. My dad's a doctor, so my brother and I . . . I guess we didn't want to disappoint him, so we worked hard too. As for my mother . . . she's my mother, and a lovely lady at that.'

He shrugged his shoulders. 'It seems ridiculous, but if Grace is who I think she is, I need your permission to tell her she's not from lowly stock as she believes.' He groaned. 'For Pete's sake, as if that matters to me!'

'But it matters very much to my daughter?'

Harry stared back at her. 'Yes. It does. And I can't bear the thought of going back to the States without taking her with me as my bride. Please, Iona. Will you help me?'

'You realise she reaches the age of maturity tomorrow? From the sixth of June onwards, she can marry whom-ever she wishes.' Iona's hand trembled as at last she raised her spoon to her lips.

'No! She never said a word. Isn't that just typical of her?'

At once he realised the crassness of his remark but Iona didn't seem to be offended. In fact, he saw a faraway look in her eyes.

'I gave that silver locket to Amy Walker

to give to Grace. One of the conditions of handing my baby over to Mr and Mrs Walker was that we wouldn't contact one another. My husband and I have never met Lord and Lady Carmichael and I had no idea both Grace's parents were dead. That's so very sad.'

'I know. It breaks my heart and for you as well as for Grace.' He reached out and grasped her hand. 'Fortunately Grace's friend Emma took on the role of substitute mother, and there's plenty of people who care about Grace, believe me. I gather she's a popular young lady both below and above stairs.'

'Thank you. You've no idea how much it means to me to hear you say that.' Iona gently withdrew her hand. 'We should at least try to eat something. The waiters are beginning to frown at our lack of appetite.' She dabbed each cheek with her white linen napkin. 'While we finish our soup, you can tell me what you want from me, Harry. Also, I'd like you to tell me all you can about my lovely daughter.'

'I'll do my best. And if it's not too painful for you, I'd be obliged if you could advise me what kind of gift is appropriate for a beautiful twenty-one-year-old woman on her special birthday.'

'You should go to Princes Street and visit Jenners' department store,' said Iona.

'Would you accompany me, my lady . . . I mean, Iona?'

'I'd like that very much,' she said. 'But maybe you shouldn't mention that I was with you when you purchased the gift you'll be handing to Grace.'

He saw the sadness in her eyes. 'I understand. May I write to you when all this is sorted out?'

'Please do, Harry. I hope and pray all will go well for you and that Grace consents to be your wife. From the little I know of your family, I think they'd take her to their hearts and provide the love and closeness I wish she could have received from me and from my own family. Grace is due to receive news of the money left in trust for her.

She may or may not wish to make use of it.' Iona swallowed hard. 'It's hardly recompense for what I did and all I can say is that my mother arranged it with the solicitors.'

Harry's sudden gulp had nothing to do with either the soup or the bread roll he was consuming.

★   ★   ★

He managed to travel back on an overnight train service though sleeping wasn't easy, with so many thoughts flitting through his head as he dissected the information received from Iona. While the train rattled southwards throughout the hours of darkness, he hoped and prayed he'd followed the right course of action. If he thought about what he'd done in a detached manner, rather than from the romantic viewpoint of a young man in love, what he saw was an American guy with a personal agenda, who'd waded in with the potential of disrupting the lives of several people.

He still didn't know whether Grace would accept his proposal, and a shiver ran down his spine as he wondered what reception he might receive from her when he turned up on the doorstep once again. He didn't even know what paperwork, as mentioned by Iona, might or might not be waiting for Grace to open on her twenty-first birthday. Logically, if she'd been given it on the death of her mother, Amy Walker, she'd already be aware of the circumstances surrounding her birth. She'd know the blood running through her veins was very different from that of the parents who'd brought her from Scotland.

So, Grace was in for the shock of her life. The circumstances of her birth certainly did explain lots of things he'd noticed about her. She had a natural elegance and even though he hadn't spent that much time in her company, when he had, she displayed an air of breeding that didn't only come from being raised in the cloistered atmosphere of a well to do, well-born London family.

Yet, Grace had this hang up about her background. He couldn't blame her for that. But he couldn't help wondering who the heck her father could have been. He hadn't dared question Iona and she'd made no mention of him. Had this person already been a married man, taking advantage of an impressionable young woman? That would point to an out-and-out cad. Or had he perhaps been someone of Iona's own age but someone she knew her parents wouldn't approve as a possible husband? He liked to think Grace had been born out of love and tenderness but maybe her paternity would always remain a secret, unless Grace took it upon herself to try and discover her true father's identity.

Harry accepted a cup of tea from the white-coated steward as the train ate up more miles. The attendant told him they were making good time and would be due into London's King's Cross Station at six thirty a.m.

He left the train with hope in his

heart and headed for the Great Northern Hotel. Carrying his overnight bag, he ordered breakfast from the sleepy waiter on duty in the dining room before heading for the gentlemen's cloakroom where he planned to restore himself to his normal clean and tidy, if a tad crumpled, self.

Sustained by a plate of scrambled eggs, sausages and bacon with toast and a large pot of coffee to prepare him for what lay ahead, Harry realised that enthusiasm alone was not sufficient reason to arrive at Seymour House before nine o'clock in the morning. Unless of course he sneaked in through the tradesmen's entrance. He decided to sit himself down in a quiet corner of the foyer and read a morning paper until at least nine thirty, by which time he reckoned the birthday girl and the rest of the household would have breakfasted and be ready to face the day.

He'd managed to order a bouquet of fresh flowers to be sent to Lady Iona with a brief message of thanks for her hospitality and a plea to say hi to her son for him. Now he wondered if he should take flowers for Lady Cressida, who he hadn't even met but who hopefully might be able to spare him a few minutes on this occasion. The very special gift he'd purchased for Grace, with a little help from Iona, reposed safely in his overnight bag.

When Harry's taxi pulled up outside Seymour House, he took a deep breath and paid his fare plus a sensible tip before climbing out, clutching a bunch of pink and white roses purchased from a florist recommended by the hotel. At this point he felt twice as nervous as he'd felt the first time he ever asked a girl if she'd care to accompany him to the movies. Seymour House at that moment appeared to be a fortress containing the girl with whom he wanted to share the rest of his life, and it took Harry several moments to calm himself before he made his way to the front door and lifted his hand to ring that formidable bell for the second time in his life.

To his relief, the door was opened not by Alfred Hicks but by a pretty young maid with a smile upon her face.

Harry dropped his case beside his feet and whipped off his hat. His other hand clasped the bouquet for her ladyship. 'Good morning,' he said. 'I'm here to see Miss Grace Walker.'

The maid blinked hard. 'Who shall I say it is, sir?'

'Harry Gresham is the name.'

'You'd better step inside, sir.'

He did so before she could change her mind. 'I'll wait here,' he said. 'Please, if it's easier, maybe you could tell Miss Rowena who's calling.'

The maid nodded and hurried towards a door at the end of the hallway. She knocked upon it and disappeared into the room. Harry reached inside his overnight bag, took out the gift, slipped it into his jacket pocket and stood waiting, hardly able to breathe. When the grandfather clock behind him struck the quarter hour, he almost jumped out of his skin.

'Mr Gresham!' Rowena was coming towards him, a welcoming smile upon her face.

'Miss Rowena, how do you do?'

'Very well indeed, thank you. Is that beautiful bouquet for Grace?'

'No, ma'am — this is for her ladyship, your mother. I do, however, have a birthday gift for Grace. Is it possible you could relieve me of these flowers in exchange for Miss Walker?'

Rowena laughed. 'It'll be a pleasure, Harry. She's upstairs but I'll fetch her before I take the flowers into the morning room. I can keep my mother occupied while you talk to Grace. Good luck!' She scampered up the staircase and ran lightly along the landing.

Harry whistled under his breath. *Come on, Grace. Come on!* If Alfred Hicks should happen along, Harry would be out the door within moments.

Or maybe not, for there was the love of his life, appearing at the top of the staircase and descending towards him while he thought his heart was on the verge of bursting with joy, or maybe with fear that he might still be rejected. She wore a simple cotton dress but to Harry, she floated down the stairs like an angel drifting to earth.

'Please come into the sitting room, Mr Gresham,' she said.

He'd lost his tongue. He followed her, having the presence of mind to hand her ladyship's bouquet to Rowena, who'd followed Grace down.

Grace closed the door behind Harry but kept her distance, her eyes wary.

Harry found his tongue. 'I'm here to wish you a very happy birthday, Grace. Congratulations. If you'll permit it, I have something to give you which I hope you'll accept.'

'Thank you, Harry. This is very kind but I really can't accept anything from you. It wouldn't be proper.'

'What the heck! What could be more proper than a man giving the girl he loves a gift on her birthday?'

She swallowed hard. 'There can be no relationship between us. I thought I made that clear.'

He took a step forward but kept his arms at his sides, even though he longed to embrace her. 'The situation's changed now. Grace, I know considerably more about you and your background than I did when we last met.'

She stood still, staring at him and, to his discomfort, her eyes had a haunted look about them. 'How can you possibly know anything about that?'

'Forgive me, my darling. When you sent me away, I arranged to visit Edinburgh. I have spoken to Lady Iona Maxwell.'

He watched Grace make a similar gesture to the one her ladyship had made at the luncheon table the day before, when she pressed her fingers to her lips.

'You know what I'm about to say. You've no doubt heard the news of your bequest and the circumstances of your birth?'

'Yes.'

'I want to put my arms around you and ask you the same question I asked before. My feelings have been the same right from the first moment I clapped eyes on you. But this time, you don't have the same excuse for turning me down.'

He watched her face contort.

'Grace, whatever is it? You've more blue blood running through your veins than I could ever dream of. Don't you love me at all? Tell me there's been some silly mix-up, please. Tell me you'll marry me and make me the happiest guy in the world.'

He moved towards her and she allowed him to put his arms around her. But she didn't hug him back. Harry froze. He had to know what bugged her. Whatever it was, he needed to convince her that everything would be all right if she'd only trust him.

'If it's Lady Cressida you're worried about, I fully intend to speak to her and make my intentions clear. You've reached the age of twenty-one, my darling. You can marry whomever you wish. Please let that someone be me!'

She gazed up at him, though she was

only a few inches shorter than he was. 'I can't bring shame on you, Harry. Despite my changed status, as you seem to regard it, the sad fact remains that my birth was illegitimate.' He saw tears glisten in the corner of each eye. 'I won't allow you to marry someone who was born out of wedlock, Harry. I won't do this to you or to your parents. I love you too much to allow you to ruin your prospects by dragging yourself into the gutter where I belong.' She whirled around, reached blindly for the door handle and fumbled with it while he rushed to her side.

'This is nonsense, Grace. For Pete's sake, this is crazy. I don't care two hoots whether your mother was married or not when she had you. Why can't you believe what I say?'

'I do believe you, Harry. I'm sure you acted in what you considered to be my best interests.'

He waited, knowing full well he wasn't going to like what followed.

'But while you may not care about

this awfulness, there are plenty of others who will.'

'We don't need to tell one single soul. We don't even have to tell my folks, if that's what you want. Marry me and let me give you a new home in America, my darling girl.'

Her wistful smile tore at his heart but something about her expression prevented him from sweeping her off her feet and carrying her away with him, regardless of what servants might say. Never mind that darned overnight bag he was sick of toting round. Nothing mattered but Grace.

He stood watching her walk away from him once more. She'd turned him down for the second time. Her gift still nestled, close to his heart, still wrapped in white tissue paper and all tied up with scarlet ribbon.

10

Outside the house, Harry hailed the first cab that came along and gave the driver his uncle Eddie's address. He threw himself onto the back seat, feeling numb. Grace had found yet another obstacle for him to surmount and he'd run out of inspiration. She'd been accepting of her lowly birth ever since she became old enough to understand the complex class system of her homeland. Now, knowing she was the daughter of a real live lady, she was so ashamed of being illegitimate that she was prepared to sacrifice the chance of happiness with him. He'd seen the look in her eyes. She couldn't hide it. She was tearing herself apart and he had no idea how to help her. Yet.

Perhaps he had one more card up his sleeve. The question was, did he dare pursue it?

Harry jumped as the cabbie announced

they were arriving at his uncle's house. He fished out a banknote and jumped out of the cab almost as soon as it came to a halt. Once inside the house, he knew exactly what he must do. Grace's natural mother must be allowed a chance to explain the missing link in this chain of events. She, above anyone else, could convince the daughter she'd been forced to give away, that she must put herself first now and not worry about other people.

Uncle Eddie left Harry alone with the telephone. Harry asked the operator for the Edinburgh number he knew off by heart and stood drumming his fingers on the carved walnut telephone table. The moment he heard Iona's clear, gentle voice across the miles, he felt his whole being thrum with hope.

Without mincing words, Harry explained Grace's reaction to the important letter she'd received. He sensed Iona's anguish. Heard her suck in her breath. He described the poignant scene with Grace, and how overwhelmed with despair he felt on hearing her determined yet unwelcome response.

'I can tell she feels the same as I do, Iona. But her decision is tearing us both apart.'

'I'm so sorry, Harry. Now tell me, am I right in thinking my daughter is what you'd probably describe as a tough cookie?'

Despite his despair, he had to laugh. The expression sounded so weird, spoken in Iona's well-modulated tones.

'I guess,' he said. 'She's mighty stubborn, that's for sure. I could use some help here, Iona. Believe me, for two pins I'd have whisked her off on my magic carpet, but she vanished before I got the chance. And I'd probably have been chased down the street by the butler and the cook and the upstairs maid and what's the other one — is it the tweeny?'

He heard Iona chuckle but when she spoke, she sounded serious. 'I hate to ask this, but you really are quite certain she feels the same about you?'

'As sure as I am that Edinburgh has a castle. Like I said, she's hurting inside just as much as I am, I'm certain of that.'

'I've already caused Grace, and now you, far too much unhappiness.' He heard a tiny sob in her voice.

'Iona, you mustn't torture yourself on that score. From what I hear, Grace had a happy, secure childhood. Mr and Mrs Walker loved her as if she were their own. And didn't I tell you how popular she is with everyone?'

'Thank you. All right, Harry. I can't stand by, knowing there are two broken hearts for which I'm responsible.'

'Apart from your own, you mean?'

He detected another stifled sob. 'Yes indeed. Now this is what you have to do. I don't for one moment think Grace would be prepared to speak to me if I were to telephone, so I intend to send her a telegram.'

He frowned. 'I'm afraid she'll tear it up, being as she's a very determined young lady.'

'Listen, Harry. I need to tell that young lady the truth around her birth. The real truth and not what she thinks she knows.'

'I don't understand.'

'You will, once Grace tells you. I'll send the telegram but you must be waiting close by and catch the boy delivering it before he rings the doorbell.'

'I can't do that! Can I?'

'Of course you can. Wait outside. When he arrives, tip him five shillings. Ask him to ring and ask for Miss Rowena. She's an ally, isn't she?'

'Well, yes.'

'Tell the boy he must deliver the telegram into her hands, and her hands only. He must also tell Miss Rowena to take the message straight to Grace. Have you got that?'

'I have. I don't know what you're up to but I'll do exactly what you say.'

'I shall be thinking of you. Now I have to go. We need to get on with this.'

Harry drove back to Manchester Square. He found a place to park and positioned himself on a seat looking towards Seymour House. He intended to keep his eyes focused on the pavement opposite and the moment he saw that uniformed telegraph boy approach, he'd make his move. He felt like a character in a spy movie but without a false beard and moustache. He didn't have a clue what Iona intended to say to Grace, but she must feel it was important — otherwise why would she make him go through this rigmarole?

Harry thanked his lucky stars it wasn't raining. He tried to look relaxed and not draw attention to himself, but he hoped no one would see him and report him for some crime like sitting on a bench and staring at a house. That would be a typically British kind of crime, he decided.

Then he saw the boy riding a bicycle, freewheeling round the corner of the gardens and whistling a cheerful song. Harry shot to his feet and strode across the road, two half-crowns clasped in one hand. Either he was going to end the day cooling his heels in a police cell, waiting for the American ambassador to bail him out, or he was going to become Grace's fiancé and therefore one very happy and fortunate man.

★   ★   ★

Rowena swallowed a mouthful of bread, dabbed her lips with her table napkin, excused herself to her mother and Grace and left the room, following in Emma's wake.

'What's all this about?' she asked Emma as soon as she closed the dining room door. 'I could see my mother wanted to stop me from leaving the table, but she daren't speak with her mouth full so I escaped.'

'There's a telegram boy on the front doorstep, Miss Rowena. He won't give what he's delivering to anyone else but you.'

'How strange. Of course I'll come, but if this is Sir Redvers playing some sort of jape, he'll need to answer to her ladyship if I get into hot water.' She marched to the open door. 'I'm the Honourable Rowena Carmichael.'

'I'm to give this to you, miss. And you're to give it to someone called Grace.'

'I don't understand. On whose instructions, pray?'

The boy stuck a thumb over his shoulder in the direction of the gardens. 'That Yankee bloke on the bench over there's the one who told me what to do.'

Rowena gazed across the road. 'Oh my goodness. Yes, very well, young man. I understand perfectly now. I imagine the gentleman tipped you?'

'Too right, miss.' He handed over the telegram. 'Ta-ra now.'

Rowena left the door open while Emma stood by, looking worried. 'Don't move one inch from this spot,' said Rowena. 'It's important Grace reads whatever this message has to say. It has something to do with Harry Gresham, because he's waiting across the way, but I have to go and stop my mother from having forty fits. I'm relying on you, Emma.'

She raced back to the dining room and disappeared inside. Moments later Grace appeared holding the telegram, a very puzzled expression on her face as she walked along the hallway.

'Emma, what's going on? Rowena said I must open this in front of you because it's important I read whatever it says. Could this be something to do with the solicitors? I don't understand.'

'Please open it, Grace. I don't know anything either but if you don't open it, you'll never know, will you?'

Grace ripped open the yellow envelope and scanned the message it contained.

DARLING GRACE STOP I WAS MARRIED TO YOUR FATHER WHEN I GAVE BIRTH STOP YOU ARE LEGITIMATE STOP MARRY HARRY STOP BE HAPPY STOP IONA X

11

Grace burst into tears and pushed the telegram into Emma's hands. 'Read that,' she sobbed. 'Tell me I'm not seeing things.'

She glanced through the doorway and saw Harry rise from the bench opposite.

Emma managed not to burst into tears. She handed the message back to Grace. 'What you read must be true. Your mother's doing the right thing by you.'

'Harry's waiting across the road,' whispered Grace.

'Then why don't you go to him?'

Grace whirled around at the sound of Rowena's voice.

'You love him,' said Rowena. 'He loves you. We can sort the rest out later.'

'So what are you waiting for?' Tears

streamed down Emma's face.

Grace gasped and shot through the doorway.

'Thank goodness, Harry has crossed the road to rescue her. She could have gone under that delivery boy's front bicycle wheel, silly girl.' Rowena stood, hands on hips, blatantly watching Grace fly into Harry's arms. She turned to Emma. 'This is so romantic! But let's leave them to it. I can't wait to hear what changed her mind, but I expect you already know.'

'If it's all right with you, Miss Rowena, I won't spoil the surprise for Grace.'

'I'll go and finish my lunch before her ladyship explodes. Thanks, Emma. I knew she'd listen to you. This is all very exciting.'

Only yards away, Grace and Harry stood on the pavement, holding on to one another as if they couldn't bear to let go.

At last he kissed her tenderly on the lips. 'I don't know what Iona said to change your mind but I'm thanking all my lucky stars that she managed it.'

'Managed what?' Grace's tone was teasing.

'Oh, darn it, I can't go down on one knee here.' Harry took her by the hand and marched her across the road without ploughing under the wheels of any oncoming vehicles.

'If you sit on that bench beneath the leafy tree, I can propose to you properly, Miss Walker.'

Grace sat down, modestly averting her eyes as Harry got down on one knee and reached for her hand.

'Would you do me the honour of becoming my wife, Grace?'

She smiled at him.

'Will this be third time lucky?'

'Yes, Harry. I can't think of anything I'd like better than to marry you.'

'You won't mind my carrying you off to New England?'

'I'll go anywhere in the world with you.'

'I love you, Grace.'

She rose from the bench while he scrambled to his feet and took her in his arms. 'I love you too, Harry.'

Grace wept quietly, while Harry, for the second time since he'd known her, provided a pristine white handkerchief.

'I hope they're tears of joy this time, my lovely girl.'

'Of course. Oh, Harry. Tell me I'm not dreaming.'

He kissed her tenderly, despite the shrill whistle sounded by a passing delivery lad on a bicycle.

'Now, I suppose I have to go and beard the dragon in her den.'

'I'd better tell you what my telegram said before you speak to Lady Cressida. I still can't believe what's happening to me.'

Grace handed Harry the message. He scanned it and whistled.

'Iona's full of surprises. But you still don't know who your father was and why she ended up marrying her cousin.'

'Maybe I never will know. It does seem odd though . . . deciding to give me away even though she was married. I wonder if it was a secret elopement and something went wrong.'

'You could always ask Iona herself.'

'I'm not sure. I'm a little wary of coming face to face with her.'

Harry laughed softly and pulled her close. 'I can assure you she's delightful. But hey, I guess I'm ruining your reputation. We can discuss what happens next after I've spoken to her ladyship. With all that's been going on, I clean forgot to give you your birthday present.' He pulled out the package from his waistcoat pocket and placed it in her hand. 'A mite later than intended, but maybe proposing before giving you this little thing is the right order to do things in.'

She pulled apart the ribbon and folded back the tissue paper to reveal a small black velvet box. He watched while she opened it.

'Harry? Oh my goodness. This isn't some little thing! This is too beautiful for words.'

'May I put it on your finger? That's where it belongs.'

She held her breath as he slipped the narrow gold band with its central sparkling diamond onto her ring finger.

Grace held out her hand to admire it. 'It fits perfectly, Harry. However did you choose the right size?'

'It wasn't difficult. You surely do take after your mother in more than one way.'

★　★　★

While Harry was closeted with Lady Cressida, Grace found Rowena and gave her the glad tidings. There was someone else Grace needed to tell and she found that someone in the courtyard, examining the engine of the Rolls Royce.

'Matt, I have something to tell you.'

He extricated himself from beneath the bonnet. 'Miss Rowena's getting married?'

'No, Matt. Actually, it's me who's getting married.' She watched expressions of surprise followed by puzzlement upon his face.

'Grace, I don't understand.'

'Don't worry, Matt. It's quite hard for me to take in too.' She held out her hand. 'I don't mean to be boastful. Please don't think that.'

Matt's face softened. He peered at the diamond and whistled. 'What a rock.'

'Well, my new fiancé does collect fossils.'

Matt threw his head back and laughed. Grace gave him a hug. 'You deserve to be happy,' he said. 'I knew deep down I wasn't the right man for you.'

Grace sensed rather than saw Polly come into the courtyard. She turned towards her. 'I'm engaged to be married, Polly. I wanted you all to know.'

The girl ran forward, eyes shining. 'I'm proper pleased, Miss Grace.'

'Thank you, Polly. Grace will do fine.'

'I reckon she will at that,' said Matt, serious once more. He held out his hand and clutched Polly's in his. 'Bet you'd like a big sparkler on your finger one day, ay, Pol?'

Grace watched the girl's cheeks turn pink. 'I imagine, if you're anything like me, Polly, you'll be happy with a ring from Woolworth's as long as you're marrying the one you love.'

'Bless you, Grace,' said Matt. 'Now I better get back to work or I'll be out on my ear and no prospect for any young lady.'

*   *   *

Two months later and only a fortnight after Emma and Alfred's quiet wedding in Marylebone, Grace and Harry were married in the village church a short distance away from Admiral's Rest and Rock Cottage. Grace chose to wear a long pearl-grey wedding dress with beading on the bodice and a silver bridal coronet upon her dark head. To Harry's delight, she wore Iona's silver locket around her neck and carried a bouquet of pink carnations mixed with sprigs of nigella and Queen Anne's lace.

Rowena, her maid of honour, wore a pale pink dress and seed pearl tiara, while carrying a smaller version of the bride's bouquet.

Lord Carmichael, who told Grace he'd never felt more honoured, gave her away. Harry's best man was Sir Redvers Fountain, the two young men having struck up an instant friendship once introduced. Red was well aware Harry's first choice had been his friend, Alexander Maxwell, from student days, but said he was pleased to stand in, knowing Alex's military duties with his Highland regiment prevented him from attending.

Grace hadn't been too sure whether she felt ready to meet her half-brother yet. Harry realised this and sympathised with her, whilst hoping that his honeymoon plan might pave the way for a future meeting. His own parents had travelled from America for the wedding and spent a few nights in Rock Cottage. His uncle Eddie drove them back to London after the wedding feast so they could spend time with him and also seize the chance to see some of the sights and visit the theatre before returning to New England. Already Grace adored her in-laws and was relieved that they felt the same about her.

When Harry first broached the idea of a honeymoon spent touring Scotland, Grace had eyed him suspiciously. 'I don't want to make things difficult for Lady Iona,' she told him while they walked hand in hand along the sea shore. Harry's parents had been invited to dine with Lord and Lady Carmichael that first evening, and the happy couple had slipped away after the meal to enjoy the sunset.

'We wouldn't just turn up on the doorstep,' Harry had insisted. 'It seems churlish to set off back to the States without at least asking her if she'd like to see us.'

Grace had remained silent.

'Darling, think what she must have gone through. It was bad enough when

I thought I might lose you forever, but what that poor woman must have suffered, having to . . . wow.'

'All right,' Grace had said. 'I don't blame her for what happened but I'd understand better if she'd been unmarried. I still can't imagine why anyone would give up their baby when they had a husband and plenty of money.'

'But this is your opportunity to find out. Express your feelings and give her the chance to explain what really happened. You deserve this, Grace, so please agree I should telephone her. We can fit Edinburgh into our itinerary once we're sure she'll be at home.'

'I can't really refuse, can I? What she did for me — for both of us — caused me to feel able to accept your proposal. But I don't expect her to justify her decision or feel bound to tell me all about my father.'

'It's obvious you're curious though, darling girl.' He squeezed Grace's hand.

'Of course I'm curious. But if she offers to have us stay with her, I don't think I can do that.'

'I'll book us a room in the hotel I used when I went to see her. How's that?'

She kissed him, taking his breath away.

★ ★ ★

Grace had never been more nervous, not even the time when she'd tiptoed through Seymour House in the small hours, dreading every creaking stair tread, knowing Rowena was unable to get back in without her help. On that occasion, Alfred Hicks had no idea someone had crept out of the house after the evening meal to attend a party. Somehow Grace had kept herself awake until she heard the stones thrown up at her window, her signal to scramble out of bed to go and unfasten the back door.

The bride and her groom had been in Scotland for a week now. They'd taken their time, stopping whenever they saw a beautiful view or took a fancy to a particular town's name. Harry had wanted to visit York on the way and after that they'd stayed in Berwick-upon-Tweed where their hotel room boasted a view of Holy Island. They'd walked hand in hand beside lochs and along historic streets, peering down alleys and admiring architecture. Harry made her laugh when he told her he'd give up the British chocolates for which he had such a fondness, if only he could discover a Scottish ancestor of his own.

Now in Edinburgh, Grace loved the hotel where Harry had stayed before, but her fingers fumbled as she tried to fasten her dress ready to dine with Lord and Lady Maxwell.

Harry came to her rescue. 'Allow me,' he said. 'I know you only married me so I could help you with stuff like this.'

She giggled. 'I don't know why I'm laughing, Harry. I really don't know how this evening's going to turn out.'

'I'd bet my last dollar Iona's feeling

even more nervous than you are, darling girl.' Gently, he turned her to face him. 'You look so beautiful. She's going to fall in love with you all over again.'

'All over again?'

'Think about it. Cut her a little slack. Imagine having to say goodbye to someone who's a part of you. Whatever the reason for her having to do that, she has to be one brave lady.'

'You're right. I'll do my best.' She closed her eyes for moments, imagining the agony of being forced to give up any child of hers and Harry's.

'That's my girl. I'll be right there with you, remember.'

'If only we knew exactly what she's told her husband.'

'Relax. She'll have come up with something. Believe me. She's had a lifetime of knowing how to handle people.'

But while the taxi pulled away from Glenbarrie House as Harry rang the doorbell, Grace needed all her reserves of determination not to head off down the crescent and leave her new husband to make her excuses.

The door opened too quickly. Grace looked anywhere but at the person opening it. Harry nudged her. She turned to find not a servant as she'd expected, but a slender, elegant woman wearing a lilac crepe dress. This woman was looking at her with such longing in her eyes that Grace knew she could only be one person.

12

Neither of them uttered a word. Grace became vaguely aware of Harry clearing his throat and suddenly Iona opened her arms and Grace fell into them, making physical contact with the woman whose existence she hadn't discovered until she became of age. She didn't know how long she and Iona had been standing there, her mother stroking her hair and crooning to her, when she heard a deep, friendly voice with a Scottish accent say, 'You must be Harry. Why don't you come and have a drink with me while our womenfolk get this over with?'

She heard Harry agree. The two men walked away and she heard Harry start chatting to Iona's husband.

Slowly, reluctantly, Iona drew back. Tears glistened upon her cheeks. 'Harry was certainly not exaggerating when he described to me how beautiful you were. You have your father's chin and nose.'

'Harry says you and I are the same shape.'

'You're taller. Not as tall as your father was of course.'

'Who was he?' The words came out before Grace could stop to think.

'The son of an earl from further north than here. Someone much older than me and a man my father detested.'

'My goodness.' The son of an earl! 'Why?' said Grace. 'Why did your father hate him so?'

'Simply because of a clan feud that began too long ago to worry about.'

'But in spite of this feud, you still married him?'

'Yes. I'd fallen in love with Donald when we met at the house of mutual friends. He made me feel as if I was the most important person in the world. I decided I wanted to become his wife and I didn't care about the conse- quences. Two close friends of his helped us wed in secret before Donald had to leave with his regiment. We had two nights together as man and wife.'

Iona smiled at Grace, who reached out to take her mother's hands in her own. 'I . . . I didn't know I was expecting a baby — expecting you — until after the sad news came of your father's death. Then I told my mother and she took over my life. Arranged for me to go away to a relation. Told me it was for the best. She insisted my father would cut me out of their lives if he found out. She also said, because no one knew apart from her, I'd stand a much better chance of making a good match if suitors perceived me as a rosebud fresh from the morning dew.'

Grace noticed the bitterness in Iona's voice. Her heart went out to the woman whose destiny had been determined by a strict mother, terrified her daughter might be deemed damaged goods. *It was for the best.* There were those words again. She shivered.

'It must have been horrible for you, losing so much and having to put a brave face on,' she said.

'It was difficult enough travelling in Europe after you were taken away to London, but coming back to live in Edinburgh and expected to attend parties and balls was a nightmare. At least I knew Amy and John would care for you.'

'They did. I've been very lucky. And thanks to you, I've married Harry and a whole new life lies ahead of me.'

Iona's eyes were sad but she smiled at her daughter. 'All I did was tell the truth when it was needed. You two had already fallen in love, but he was devastated at the thought of losing you.'

Iona took her daughter by the hand and led her towards the drawing room. The men's laughter percolated into the hallway.

'Andrew, my husband, is a good man. As cousins, close in age, we were part of the same social circle, of course. He watched me trying to act as though I hadn't a care in the world until one day he arrived and took me out to lunch. I opened my heart to him and told him I was afraid I could never fall in love again. He looked at me across the table and said he couldn't bear the thought of me marrying someone else and he thought he had enough love for both of us.'

'Oh,' Grace said. 'What a wonderful thing to say.'

'Wasn't it? I accepted his proposal knowing it would please my parents, but I never dreamed how much I'd grow to love him. The birth of Alexander helped of course, although hardly a day went by but I didn't think of you.'

'I know Harry wants me to meet Alexander some day. I'm not sure I feel ready yet.'

'I understand. My son is Harry's friend so it's natural he wants to show you off. I need to tell Alex about you though. It's not fair he doesn't know, now the secret's out.'

'That sums up how I feel about Harry. I thought I'd been stupid to assume the name of Maxwell when he and I first met. But my lack of thought has resulted in more change than I'd ever have imagined possible.'

'We have such a lot to catch up on,' said Iona.

'I want to tell you what happened to my mother and father.'

Iona nodded. 'Amy and John deserve to hold a special place in my memory and in yours. Now, come.'

But Grace hesitated in the doorway as Iona entered the room. The men rose immediately and Iona turned and placed an encouraging arm around Grace's shoulders.

'Little did I know,' said Iona, 'that when our son brought you to visit us, Harry, you would one day become the link between me and the daughter I never thought to see again. I shall never be able to thank you enough.'

THE END

We do hope that you have enjoyed reading this large print book.

Did you know that all of our titles are available for purchase?

We publish a wide range of high quality large print books including:
Romances, Mysteries, Classics
General Fiction
Non Fiction and Westerns

Special interest titles available in large print are:
The Little Oxford Dictionary
Music Book, Song Book
Hymn Book, Service Book

Also available from us courtesy of Oxford University Press:
Young Readers' Dictionary
(large print edition)
Young Readers' Thesaurus
(large print edition)

For further information or a free brochure, please contact us at:
Ulverscroft Large Print Books Ltd.,
The Green, Bradgate Road, Anstey,
Leicester, LE7 7FU, England.
Tel: (00 44) 0116 236 4325
Fax: (00 44) 0116 234 0205

I'M WATCHING YOU

Susan Udy

Lauren Bradley lives a quiet life in her village flat, with only her cat for company. So why would anyone choose her as a target for stalking? As the harassment becomes increasingly disturbing, several possible candidates emerge. Could it be Lauren's old friend, Greg, who now wants more than just friendship? Sam, the shy man who works in the butcher's shop across the street and seems to know her daily routine? Or even handsome but ruthless Nicholas Jordan, her new boss to whom she is dangerously, but hopelessly, attracted?

FAIRLIGHTS

Jan Jones

The fortified pele tower of Fairlights, its beacon shining out across the harbour, has guarded Whitcliff for centuries. Sorcha Ravell thought she'd recruited the perfect restoration expert in Nick Marten — but he turns out to be dangerously attractive; knows more about her than she can account for; and is very, very angry. As the autumn storms build and the tension rises, Sorcha must overcome a paralysing physical fear and confront a terrifying mental enigma. What happened to her so many years ago? And why can she not remember?

DIFFICULT DECISIONS

Charlotte McFall

Tracy Stewart left the Derbyshire village of Eyam to pursue her dream of becoming a solicitor. Returning home for Christmas is the last thing she wants to do. A brush with Mike O'Neill starts to change her mind, but is it enough to make her stay? Mike has taken over running his father's bookshop, whilst working as a writer in secret. But can he keep his secret as well as the girl he loves?

TANGLED WEB

Pat Posner

After his beloved great-uncle has an angina attack, Jarrett tells his fiancée, Emily, that the elderly man's one wish is to live long enough to see him happily married. Emily agrees to bring their wedding forward but she's devastated when, on their honeymoon, she hears of a clause in Jarrett's great-uncle's will: the first baby boy born in the family will inherit the family business. Has Jarrett only married her so he can produce an heir before either of his brothers beat him to it?